FORBIDDEN FATES

KJHART

Forbidden Fates by KJHart

Published by: Kindle Direct Publishing

kjhartbooks@gmail.com

ISBN: 9798848270105

1st Edition

Dedication:

To my family and friends who have always been there for me. I couldn't have made it here without you. Much love.

ONE:

JOURNIE

"I can't believe it's your first year of college!" My mom exclaims as I let out a huff. She lifts a hand and ruffles my hair, lightly caressing my cheek.

She was clearly more excited than I was. I smile as I pull her into a hug. "I'm nervous." I say, pulling away to chew on my fingernails. For the first time, I was going all the way to New York City without my mom. Nervous was a complete understatement.

"Stop that! You will be fine." She muses, throwing the last of my belongings into my trunk. Granted, it was only two hours away from where I currently lived, but my anxiety had my thoughts haywire. I didn't like change, but I knew if I wanted to become something, this was the best way.

"Call me when you get there!" I climb into my car, feeling my mom's lips on my cheek.

"Oh, you will hear from me tons." I say, locking my seatbelt and closing the door. I hoped my trusty old Honda would get me there safely.

I pull my long blond locks into a messy bun and put my car in reverse.

FORBIDDEN FATES

I sighed heavily as I looked at my lifelong home and the nervousness swept over me once again.

"I love you!" My mom shouts and I wave my hand at her, backing out of the driveway.

An hour and a half later, I found myself on the side of the road and tears threatening to fall. It would just be my luck that this would happen, while I was completely alone. I fought back a wave of nausea as I pulled my phone from my bag, ready to call the police. As I was about to hit dial, a car pulled in behind me. My heart rate instantly sped up, hoping it was someone decent and not a creepy serial killer. My mind went to the worst scenario.

A light knock came at my window and my jaw almost hit the floor when I see the man before me. Even with sunglasses blocking his eyes I could tell he was very attractive. A small stubble gathered on his face and his lips were full and ready for a kiss. I laugh at myself and open my door slightly. He didn't look harmful.

“Are you okay?" Was the first question out of his mouth. I shrug my shoulders. Opening my door, I let my words spill out.

"I was just driving and it started sputtering, so I pulled over and it completely shut off." I say, deciding that I could trust this man enough, he didn't look much older than I.

"Pop your hood." I oblige and watch as he wiggles some around on my battery and then pops a cap. I watch as his eyes squint, trying to see into the tiny tube.

"Looks like you're out of water ma'am."
He walks to his car and comes back with a jug of water. How convenient. I can't help but watch as his muscular frame pours the water in, and he gives me a thumbs up. I twist the key and it instantly roars to life. I sigh in relief. I step back out of my car and almost want to give him a hug. "Thank you so much!" I say as he smiles at me. As if I weren't already hot enough, my cheeks flooded with warmth. I take a deep breath before continuing,
"It's actually my first time driving to New York by myself, I'm starting my first semester of college tomorrow."
"No problem! I know how scary that can be, I'm glad I was able to help! Maybe I'll see you around." I smile at this statement and fate willing, maybe I would.
As soon as I was back on the road, I called my mom letting her know the mishap and that I would hopefully be at my new apartment within the hour. I was ready to relax.
Finally arriving to my apartment, I lugged all my things inside, wishing I had some help. After what seems like forever, I decided to have a pizza delivered and relax while watching Netflix. Tomorrow was quite possibly the biggest day of my.As I lay in my bed, my thoughts drift to the hot stranger and I wonder if I will ever get to see him again.The next morning, I wake with a start, remembering where I was and jumped from bed.I quickly got dressed and threw on jeans and a t-shirt, making my way to campus.Thankfully it was only about ten minutes from my apartment. Once I arrived, I almost sprint to my first class, realizing I only had

five minutes left for attendance verification.
I settle into my seat; and look up when the doors shut. My eyes almost bulge from my head as I see who stands in front of the classroom. It was the man who helped me with my car.
I couldn't believe it. His eyes scan the room and then land on me. I can see the shock on his face as well. I was right about one thing; he was *very* attractive without his sunglasses.

TWO:

JOURNIE

My eyes followed him the whole lecture. I tried to look away, especially when his eyes would find mine, but I couldn't. I was captivated by his eyes. It was nearly impossible. I had only spoken with him a short time and already felt a spark there. Maybe it was because he was the first one to help me since being here.

"Ms. Derringer, care to see me?" My eyes snapped over to his for the hundredth time and my heart sped up. I nod my head and realize that the classroom was already empty. I gather my stuff and walk up to his desk.

"How's that car?" I shrug, I hadn't had the chance to drive since yesterday.

"As far as I know, it's good as new." I nervously laugh, adjusting my backpack on my shoulder. I watch as he scribbles something down on a piece of paper. Once I take it from him, I realize it's his number. I shove it into my pocket, my cheeks heating up.

"Just in case your car breaks down, or you, whichever happens first." He winks and I laugh. He was very forward.

"I know how stressful it can be moving away from what you've known your whole life." I nod and smile at him. As wrong as it already was, I found a bit of comfort in his forwardness.

"Thanks Mr. Bennett, it's very scary moving to a town you know very little about." He smiled at me one final time before I left the room. I made my way back to my apartment, heart racing and thoughts running wild. Why did I feel this way? He was a good-looking man but is my professor and *strictly* off limits.

I change into more comfortable clothes and relax on my bed, which is still in the living room. I hadn't had the time to set up my bedroom yet. I went to grab a bottle of water from the fridge and realized I hadn't made that dreaded first grocery trip.

I sigh loudly and grab my keys, no better time than the present to test my car.

Once I arrive to the store, all in one piece, I gather a cart and curse silently as I forgot my list. I tried to scrape my deepest thoughts for what I had written down, but only got a few things I thought were necessary. Bread, lunch meat, water, and some snacks. There was a ton of fast-food places near me, so I wouldn't be going without. Satisfied with my choices, I go to check out and remember I had Mr. Bennett's number.

The battle within me roared as I thought about letting him know my car was fine or just to keep it how it is and tell him Wednesday. Once I got back to my apartment

I decided that texting him was the way to go. Probably not the best idea. I've been told I'm the queen of impulse decisions.

-Thanks to you, my car is working as good as new. -J

Within seconds, I receive a message back. Should I open it right away? I wait a few moments before unlocking my screen. Once my eyes scanned the message, I feel a smile appear on my face.

-Good to hear! How about you? -A

I bite my lip and sit down on my bed,

-so far so good. -J

The minutes rolled on and I hadn't gotten a reply, I figured it was probably for the best. I didn't need to start out my first semester of college texting my professor, but fate seemed to have it that way.

Or maybe it was my lack of judgement, who knew. I pulled my blanket to cover my face and let out a long breath.

I needed to sort through my thoughts and wake with a fresh mind. Just before falling asleep, I call my mom to update her on my first day.

Leaving out the details of how the guy who helped me get my car back on the road was my professor. And the fact that he was super delicious.

THREE:

JOURNIE

Wednesday couldn't get here fast enough. I found myself wanting to message Mr. Bennett again, but I somehow resisted that urge. Maybe it was because I knew I would see him soon. I looked in the mirror at my outfit, a black skirt with a white tank and a cropped blue jean jacket.
I looked down at my combat boots and hoped it went well together, considering it was the middle of August. I threw my hair back into a messy bun and applied little makeup on my face. My heart raced in anticipation of his class, and I hoped I would be able to have a conversation with him.
I began walking over to campus, keeping my head down and AirPods blasting in my ears. Music was my go-to when I needed to calm my nerves. I was only nineteen and I knew plenty of others who dealt in different ways.
I check the time on my phone and realize I'm going to get to class early and decide to stop by the cafe to grab a breakfast sandwich and coffee. I felt my phone buzz in my pocket, and I pulled it out. Mr. Bennett's name was across my screen. I tried to hide my smile but failed. What if he were watching me?

-nice sandwich you have there. -A
I quickly turn around, trying not to cause any unwanted attention to myself and spot him sitting on a bench outside. He was alone and I took the opportunity to make my way over. Students talk to teachers outside of the classroom all the time, right?
"It is very good." I say and take a bite as I sit down next to him. He shifts in his spot as he looks over at me.
"It looks delicious." Yeah, like you. I want to say aloud and mentally curse myself for even thinking that. I almost choke on my next bite. I take a deep breath.
“Are you alright?" I nod at him and take a sip of my coffee. Wrong move. It goes down the wrong way and I fall into a coughing fit. Leave it to me to make things awkward.
"Good as ever." I reply once my coughing fit is over. He tosses a smile my way and I melt into a puddle on the ground. I take in his appearance. He had a light stubble on his features and dressed in a black t shirt and jeans, he looked ready to devour. I must have been paying too much attention to him because the next thing I know, my coffee is now all over my shirt.
"Crap!" I exclaim, jumping up. I quickly try to pat at my shirt as I feel hands on mine.
"Here take this." I am handed a flannel shirt, two sizes too big.
"Thank you so much!" I say as I rush off towards the bathroom to change. Great. Now I've embarrassed myself even more.

Could I be anymore awkward?

Once I toss my ruined tank and jacket into my backpack, I look at myself in the mirror. I loved the way his shirt fit my shape, even though it almost swallowed me whole. There was just something about it being his. It smelled of a sweet and tangy scent and I let it consume my senses. I already loved his cologne.

I toss my backpack over my shoulder and make my way to his class. I'm not sure I'd be able to focus much today, but I would try my best.

He smiles at me as I enter the room and I grow weak in my knees. I find the closest desk and take a seat. English wasn't exactly my best subject but having Mr. Bennett as my professor would make it bearable.

During the lecture, I couldn't help but zone him out and daydream. My eyes followed his frame as he walked in front of the room, I wanted nothing more than to have my body wrapped around his.

At that thought, I could feel my cheeks become red.

His eyes wandered over to mine many times and he'd always give a small smile.

It's like he knew what I was thinking. By the end of the lecture, my pen cap was chewed, and I was having thoughts about my professor that no student should have.

FOUR:

AIDEN

I couldn't lie, seeing her walk into my classroom, with my shirt on had me feeling a way no professor should be feeling about a student. I try to brush the thought off, but it stayed in the back of my mind the whole lecture. I'd find my eyes locking with hers and seeing a small smile appear on her sinful lips.

They looked so soft, so tempting. She was so innocent, and it ignited something deep inside of me. Something I hadn't felt before. In my two years of teaching, I had never felt this way about a student, much less a younger one. I told myself I never would.

I was only twenty-seven, so not much older than her. I resisted the urge to ask her to stay after class, not wanting to call much attention to us. Us. Was that even a thing? I'd only known her for a few short days. And felt something I haven’t felt in years.

Everything rational in my adult brain has flown out of the window at this point. As long as I didn't bring my thoughts into reality, everything would be okay. If I can just wait until the semester is over and she isn't my student anymore, then I could.

I bite down on my lip. Instant attraction was a thing, and I hadn't fully experienced it until my eyes landed on her, on the side of the road.

Once all my lectures were over, I made my way towards home, a nice cold drink calling my name. The more I drank, the more texting her sounded like a good idea. I glanced at the clock, it was already past ten and I'm sure she was in bed. Screw it.

-keep the shirt, it looks better on you. -A

Too forward? Maybe so. I toss my phone on the bed beside me, knowing after that, there is no turning back. The liquid courage was a terrible idea. Pair it with my inability to resist temptation and it was sin city. It's doubtful she will even reply.

I had to calm my racing heart as my phone buzzed beside me. I instantly picked it up, opening her reply.

-it's a new personal favorite. - J

My fingers hover over my keyboard, wanting to reply but deciding it wasn't the best idea. I place my phone on charge and thought about how great it would feel to have her next to me.

I shake the thought from my head and to no avail, my mind wanders to her lips. So tempting and forbidden. Somehow, that made me want it even more. I didn't want to jeopardize my career, but there was always the option of finding another university to teach at. I shook my head.

I made a promise to myself to not act on my thoughts until she wasn't in my class.

It was wrong. So wrong. Then why did it feel so right? Why did I feel like risking it all just to have her? I drift off to sleep, Journie prominent on my mind.

FIVE:

JOURNIE

"Hey mom!" I say excitedly, pulling her into a hug The weekend was finally here. I could relax and get my things in order at my apartment. My mom volunteered to come up and help me finish. For that, I was thankful. The first week was stressful, and then I had conflicting feelings about my professor. Not the way I had imagined my week to go.

"Hey sweetie. I'm so glad to see you!" She kissed my cheek lightly, grabbing a box from my kitchen floor and bringing it to my bedroom.

I had at-least managed to get my bed set up in there and a couch in the living room. Once we got everything set up, I sat across beside my mom on the couch, glad to have some familiarity around me. She clears her throat.

"Any cute boys yet?" I almost spit my drink out and shake my head.

"No, not yet." I reply, my mind going to Mr. Bennett. His dreamy blue eyes distracting me. I try to push the thought aside and focus on my mom. She could read me enough to know when I was keeping something.

"When I was in college, I met the love of my life."

She smiled, closing her eyes to remember. I gave her a sad smile; I never knew my dad. He died before I could remember any part of him.
"I wish I could have had more time with him." I whisper, bringing her into a hug.
"Me too baby." She hugged me a bit tighter, and I savored the feeling. I had the closest bond with her, and I didn't like to hold anything back.
"Talk to me when you are ready." She winked, pulling me into her chest.
I knew I couldn't get away with her not knowing anything.
"It's complicated." I huff, nuzzling my neck into her chest. There was nothing like the comfort of your mother.
“Are you sure it’s for you then?” She asks, pulling away to look into my eyes.
"Are you hungry?" I ask, avoiding her question.
“Ms. Journie Grace, are you avoiding my question?” I shrug and she laughs.
“I’m starving.” She replies,
"I can door dash Chinese?" I ask, hopefully she would agree. She gave me a sly look, holding onto her stomach.
"Anything for you." She half smiles. I loved her so much.

"Are you sure you're okay with swapping these classes around?" I nod my head. Anything to be closer to him. I was a student aid on Tuesdays and Thursdays for the science professor, but suddenly got swapped to Tuesdays

Not that I was complaining, or anything.
I had ten minutes before I had to be there, and I was taking any time that I could to calm my nerves.
"No problem at all!" I smile, grabbing papers from the assistant's hand and making my way over to Mr. Bennett's classroom. I lightly knock on the door before entering and his head snaps up to me.
"Ms. Derringer, what a nice surprise." He grins, motioning for me to come in. It felt like he could hear my heartbeat inside of my chest.
"You can shut the door behind you." He nods at the door. I'm not sure it's the best idea but I wasn't going to argue. I sit my backpack down and go over to close the door. I could feel the tension between us as soon as I walked into the door.
"So, what can I do to help?" I ask and he looks at me his eyes darkening. I feel my cheeks become flushed and I try to hide my smile.
He places his pen on the desk and gives a big sigh. He leans back in his chair, his eyes boring back into mine.
"You can help me organize some files, if you'd like." He says and points to a shelf full of boxes.
"Your wish is my command." I say and get up going to the shelf. I could hear him intake a sharp breath, and I knew then that those simple words made him feel a certain way. I bit down on my lip to keep from giggling, I could have some fun with this.
Today probably wasn't the best day to wear a skirt, but I had no idea when I put it on.

I would have to stretch in-front of Mr. Bennett to reach some files.

I could feel his eyes on me as I climb into a chair and reach up to grab a box. I almost lose my balance and laugh at myself, hopping down from the chair. His eyes are on me as I walk towards the front of the room. He gets up from his chair and walks over towards me. I jump a little when I feel his hand cover mine. His daring blue eyes stare into my green ones, filled with things to say. He lowers his voice.

"Do you think wearing a skirt is a good idea?" His voice is breathy, and I can almost feel it on my face. A minty scent washes over me, filling my nostrils. I was about to be putty in-front of this man.

"Is there something wrong, Professor Bennett?" I ask, taking my hand away from his. He narrows his eyes at me.

“Do you like teasing for fun?" He asks, taking a step away from me, his gaze never leaving mine.

"Me? Teasing? No way." I giggle and take a seat. I begin sorting through the papers, my mind racing knowing he is in-front of me. Suddenly the papers are taken from me, and I stand up. Startled.

"I think you are." He breathes, taking a step closer to me. My heart is pounding in my chest. Were we about to kiss? My mind couldn't grasp the fact that this was very wrong. In this very moment, I didn't care. He reaches out and strokes my cheek, shivers run down my spine. I've never kissed a man before and I wanted to know what it felt like.

I closed the gap in between us, standing on my tip toes.
I gently press my lips to his as a groan escapes his lips. He brings his hand around to cup my neck, pulling me closer to him. I open my mouth and our tongues tangle together, lapping each other up.
I press myself into him harder, so that nothing could fit in between us. He pushes me back onto the desk, as the box of papers fall to the floor. I jump away from him, somehow biting his lip in the process. I bend down to pick up the papers, my heart racing and mind going haywire.
"I'm so sorry!" I apologize, looking into his eyes. He brings a hand up to his hair, running it through his brown locks. He lets out a breathy sigh and goes to sit back at his desk. He's not looking at me when I come back over, but instead studying a paper.
"I think you should go." He whispers, still not looking up to meet my eyes. I nod my head, tears threatening to spill over.
"Okay. I'm sorry " I apologize again, leaning down to pick up the remaining papers.
"Leave it." He says and I nod my head once more. My heart was still pounding, and I couldn't help the tears that escaped my eyes as I left his room. Who was I to think that he wanted to kiss me? Who was I to think that a man like him couldn't ever want a girl like me? Who was I to think that kissing my professor was a good idea in the first place?
Once I got to my apartment, I collapsed onto my bed stuffing my face into the pillow.

I let more tears fall from my eyes as I made a promise to myself. To never be that vulnerable around him again.

SIX

JOURNIE

Two weeks. Two whole weeks have passed since I made the mistake to kiss Mr. Bennett. Sure, we've had light conversations and professional ones at that, but I feel like he's avoiding me. I knew I shouldn't have kissed him, but my judgement hasn't always been the best.

I waltz into his classroom like nothing has happened, except for today, I am trying to capture his attention.

I paired his flannel shirt with a black skirt and my combat boots. I pulled my hair back into a messy bun and applied a little more makeup than usual.

I left his shirt open, with my white crop tank under. I hoped it was captivating enough. I go in and shut the door behind me, catching his attention immediately.

His eyes snap up to mine, instantly raking over my body. His eyes traveled to look at my lips and then my chest. Bingo.

"Good afternoon, Mr. Bennett." I say as I take my seat.

"Good afternoon, Ms. Derringer." He nods at me, his eyes never leaving mine. I watch as his tongue darts out to wet his lips and I tear my eyes away.

The memory of them covering mine had my mind in a frenzy. I wanted nothing more than to have that feeling again.
"What do you need me to do today?" I ask, taking a strand of my hair that had fallen, twirling it with my finger. I watch as he bites down on his lip.
"Not much, unless you want to organize more files." He suggests.
"Sure thing." I say, spotting a box at the top of the shelf. This should be fun. I place my backpack on the desk beside me and go towards the bookshelf.
I prop myself up in a chair and try to reach it, but I fail. I grumble out of frustration and place my foot on the second shelf. After gaining some sort of balance, I place my other foot on the shelf and begin reaching for the box. Next thing I know, I am falling, and a strong pair of arms catch me.
"You almost gave me a heart attack." Wildfire shoots through me as his hands fall on my waist, steadying me. Not removing his hand, I take the opportunity to step closer to him. I can hear his breathing slow and I'm sure mine matched his.
"Why have you been ignoring me?" I say softly, looking into his eyes. He lets out a long sigh and places his finger under my chin. He swallows hard before speaking.
"It's wrong, Journie. On so many levels." I feel my eyes water up. I didn't want to cry in front of him. I jerk my head away from him and a tear slips from my eyes. I feel a soft hand under my chin, turning my head so that I'm

facing him again.

Testing the waters, I place my hand on the back of his neck and bring my lips to the base of his neck. I place a soft kiss there, earning a groan from him.

"Does this feel wrong?" I ask, trailing my kisses lower. He opens his mouth to speak and nothing, but a groan comes out. I can't help the smirk that settles onto my lips as I pull away.

I could feel his heart beating out of his chest and I knew then he felt the same way.

"Just as I thought." I say, backing away from him.

He takes a hand and runs it through his hair.

"I'm not good at resisting temptation Journie." He steps away from me, and I can see his hands trembling.

"How about we talk over dinner?" This question surprises me.

"Yeah, that sounds good." I say, looking up to see a small smile on his face.

"I'm sorry for being such a jerk, I don't know how to deal with things properly." He apologizes, pulling me into his arms. I feel as if I could stay there forever.

"Are you ready?" He asks as I grab my backpack. I nod my head and follow him out of the door.

SEVEN:

JOURNIE

I walk behind Mr. Bennett into his place, my heart pounding ferociously. I try to steady my breathing as I take off my shoes, following him into his kitchen.

"So, what're you feeling?" He asks and I shrug. I'm sure he is an amazing cook.

"Chicken Alfredo?" I ask, taking a seat at his table. It is decorated lightly, like I expected. My eyes travel over to a table filled with pictures. He looked very happy.

"That happens to be my expertise." He smiles, rolling up the sleeves on his shirt. I watch as he pulls chicken breasts out of the freezer and suddenly, I feel the need to help.

"Can I help?" I ask, standing up. He nods over to a cabinet.

"Be my guest." I smile and go over to the cabinet grabbing the noodles.

"Pots are under there." He points to a cabinet.

"Thanks!" I loved cooking myself, I haven't had the time since I've moved into my apartment. I could make a killer lasagna.

Once the meal is put together, I shovel it into my mouth.

"Someone must be starving." He winks and I almost choke on a noodle. If only he knew.

"It's the first thing I've had to eat all day." I watch as he eyes me, his gaze darkening. I couldn't help the feeling that stirred deep down inside of me.

"I can't wait for dessert." I watch as he bites down on his lip, looking into my eyes.

"Oh yeah, what's that?" I ask, ice cream sounded delicious. Or him. That would be great too.

"I was thinking a sundae." I smile.

"So was I!" I exclaim, finishing the last bites of my Alfredo. I get up to help him with the dishes, but he demands I sit back down.

For once, I listen and watch as he cleans up. My eyes followed his every movement and I wanted to touch his every muscle. I tried to focus on my phone to distract myself, but he hovered front and center on my mind.

"What are you thinking about?" I jump slightly and look up. He is standing directly in-front of me, eyes blazing into mine.

"Truth or a lie?" I ask. After all, the whole reason I'm here is because we had to talk. He sighed heavily.

"Truth. Of course."

"You." I say simply and I watch as he brings a hand up and rakes it though his hair. He turns his back to me.

"Journie..." he trails, turning back around to face me.

"If you weren't my student, things would be different." I stand up, I knew I shouldn't have come here.

"Yeah, but I am."

I reply, making a move to grab my backpack. I sling it over my shoulder and begin walking over to the door.

"Journie, Wait." He called, moving closer towards me.

"What? If I'm just your student, then I really shouldn't be in your house." I say, turning around and placing my hand on the doorknob.

I could just walk home. I felt a hand cover mine just as I was about to twist the knob. I take a deep breath and turn around.

"I need to leave." I say as he takes a hand and slides my backpack from my shoulder. It hits the floor with a loud thud, and I jump a little.

He brings his hand out and touches my cheek, my heart beating fast in my chest.

"I told you I'm not good at resisting temptation."

He whispers, crashing his lips to mine. I let out a small moan, brining my hands to wrap around his neck. I pull him closer to me, not wanting this moment to end. I have him exactly where I wanted him.

He grabs my thighs and wraps them around his waist. I push myself deeper into him, feeling him against me. I was done for. There was no way I could ever recover from this. I groan when his lips leave mine and begin to trial kisses down my neck.

"You can't leave, we haven't had dessert yet." He whispered heavily in my ear. A chill runs down my spine. He pulls away from me, pulling me into his arms.

"Oh yeah, what's that?" I ask, still hopeful for the ice cream.

"You." He says simply and I gasp.
"Mr. Bennett," I begin, but he quickly interrupted.
"Kidding. As great as that would be," He trails, pausing to wet his lips.
"Ice cream it is." I follow him back to the kitchen. He sets a bowl in front of me, and I dig in. My heart was still pounding from our earlier actions. I hoped he wouldn't run away this time.
"Are you going to ignore me for two weeks now?" I ask, looking into his eyes.
"I barley could for that long. No way." He said, leaning down to place a kiss on my forehead. My insides melt.
"Good to know." I say and place my bowl in the sink.
"I really should get going though, I need to study." I say and look at the time.
"I'll drive you." Mr. Bennett suggests, and I nod, picking my backpack up from the floor.
“Thanks Mr. Bennett.”
"Call me Aiden, please." He says as we walk out the door. A smile appears on my face.
"Okay, Aiden." I say and get comfortable in his car. This was not how I pictured my college days going, but at this moment in time, I couldn't picture it any other way.

EIGHT

AIDEN

That was it. I am completely done for. All my adult reasoning has left my body and here I am like a lost puppy dog.

The second that I pulled over to help Journie on the side of the road, I knew she was something. I kicked myself for not asking for her number that day. But fate had its role and placed her in my class the very next morning.

As I kissed her against my door, all the things that was wrong with what we were doing bounced around in my head, but in that moment the only thing that mattered was that she was against me. I needed more. Craved more.

I knew our relationship was wrong, and only because she was my student.

I knew I needed to refrain myself from her and I succeeded for two weeks, two long agonizing weeks. I doubt I could go any longer. I didn't plan too, but I knew we needed to keep it at a minimum. If I weren't careful, I could lose my job. I knew if it got too hot and heavy, I could resign, although I really did like teaching at NYU.

But if I could finally have the love of my life, then I would see it worth. If only we could make it through these next

FORBIDDEN FATES

It was never my plan to fall for a student, but I have a feeling Journie will have me bending all sorts of rules.

As I got ready for my lecture, I realized it was Thursday and I had Journie as my aid. I hadn't had any kind of physical contact with her since the ordeal at my house, and I needed her desperately.

Sure, we have texted each other, but that didn't suffice. I needed her in my arms.

As the day drug on, I checked the clock several times, hoping that four would make it here quickly.

A soft knock came at my door and my heart began to speed up. I knew it was her just by how she knocked. Even that was graceful.

"Come in." I say, getting up from my seat. Once she made it safely into my room, I shut the door behind her and locked it.

I watched as she sat her things on the desk, her gaze moving over to me. I watched as she bit down on her full lip. I lost all self-control. I walked over to her, bringing her into my arms. She melted into me instantly.

"Hello there beautiful." I greeted, as I placed a soft kiss on her neck. She smiled, lifting my head up.

She placed a kiss on my lips as I pulled her in tighter. A light groan escaped my lips as I pushed her back against the desk. The things this woman does to me. I couldn't get enough.

Our tongues intertwined with each other, leaving my heart pounding. I pressed myself against her as she wrapped her thighs around my waist.

I needed her to be closer. I broke away from her lips only for a moment to trail kisses down her neck.

"Aiden..." she breathed, bringing her hand up and running it through my hair. I groaned louder this time, knowing I needed to stop before it got too out of hand.

As much as I would love to have her, I knew this wasn't the place I wanted to take her. I pulled away regrettably, placing a soft kiss on her forehead.

"As much as I was enjoying that," I begin, looking at her swollen lips and swipe my finger across them.

"We need to stop before I really can't control myself." I say, keeping her against my chest.

I could feel her breathing hard against me.

Knowing I had that effect on her drove me insane. I could see a pout form on her lips,

"Is something wrong?" I ask, worried that I had done something.

"Yes," she spoke softly, pulling away from me. My heart dropped.

"I didn't want to stop." She finishes, and I smiled.

"One day we won't have too." I say and place a soft kiss on her cheek. She was going to be the death of me.

NINE:

JOURNIE

Twirling my pen between my fingers, I watch as his muscular body walks across the room. I was squirming in my seat. Every glance held passion and lust. I couldn't wait to crash my lips to his.

He was the only friend I had made since coming here and I was totally okay with that. I didn't have to worry about a roommate to bug me with questions or wondering where I am at night.

Three weeks had passed since he kissed me against his door, and I absolutely could not get enough. I hadn't told my mom any details yet, but she does know I am seeing someone a little bit older than me.

"Ms. Derringer?" I snap out of my gaze quickly. My eyes find his and I see him smirking at me.

"See me after class?" I nod, trying not to draw too much attention to us.

"Yes, sir." I say and look down at my notes. The end of class couldn't get here fast enough. When twenty minutes have finally passed, I stayed in my seat. I hoped I didn't do anything wrong.

Once everyone cleared the classroom, he waited a minute to make sure the hallway was clear.

He had an hour before his next class began. He closed the door and turned to me, smirking.

"Care to visit me?"

"Aiden..." I trail, getting up from my seat.

"I want to show you something." I raise an eyebrow.

"What could that be?" I question, standing in-front of him.

He goes around to stand behind me, and I turn around.

He's grinning at me now as he places his hands on my shoulders, pushing me backwards.

My back hits the cool board, sending shockwaves throughout my entire body.

"We can't." I try to reason, all the while bringing my hands to clasp around his neck. A smirk plays at his lips.

"But we can." He whispers against my neck. All my self-control slips, and I am vulnerable under his touch. The instant his lips meet my neck, a moan escapes my lips. Who knew that something so wrong could feel so...right?

"Aiden," I moan, wrapping my arms tighter around him.

He grabs my thigh and wraps it around his waist, pulling me closer to him.

"Aiden, you have a class soon." I say in between breaths.

"Baby, we still have an hour." He pulls away from my neck and places his lips softly onto mine.

I knew there was no chance in arguing so I obliged. I pressed my lips hard onto his, pushing my hips closer to his.

I hear a groan escape from his lips and can't help but smile. It was like music to my ears.
"Someone could find us." I say, pulling away only for a moment to kiss his neck.
"Let them." He groans, rocking his hips back and forth. I gasp and throw my head back. It was a feeling like I've never had before. The only way to describe it was euphoric.
"Aiden," I try to reason again, wrapping my thighs tighter around him.
"We have to stop." I say, bringing his lips back to mine.
"You don't know how irresistible you look in my shirt. I wanted to rip it off you the second I laid eyes on you." I laugh slightly at this, as he retreats, regretfully from me.
"Another time." I say as he places a kiss on my forehead.
"How am I supposed to get through the rest of the day without your touch?" He whisperers, looking deep into my eyes.
"You will." I say as a knock comes at the door. We both jump apart as I quickly button my shirt back up.
I run my fingers through my hair to smooth it down and notice Aiden has lipstick smeared on his face. I laugh, wetting my finger and wiping it from his chin.
"That will be a dead giveaway." I say and walk over to grab my things. I place a random paper in my hand and walk over to his desk, pretending to be asking him a question.
Come in!" He yells and the door swings open.

"Hey Mr. Bennett, can I ask you a few things?" A boy asks and I am very thankful he doesn't notice me right away. As soon as I think that his eyes dart to me.

"If you are busy, I can come back." The boy says, starting to back out.

"No, no. Come on you are fine. Ms. Derringer we can finish this later, okay?" Aiden says and hands the blank piece of paper back to me. Our hands touch and electricity shoots through me.

"Yes, sir." I mumble, my heart still racing. That was too close. We had to be more careful. We didn't need to touch each other at school, as hard as that was going to be.

TEN:

JOURNIE

As my mother sits across from me, I bounce my leg up and down. I was extremely nervous for her to be here; I couldn't take the guilt any longer and had to tell her I was seeing my professor.

I only had a little over two months left of this semester and thankfully, we had hidden it well so far.

I told my mom absolutely everything, she deserved to know this. I have given her a few hints and honestly, she has probably pieced it together by now. She was always gushing about how she couldn't wait until I met 'the one'.

I invited Aiden over to dinner and albeit, it may not be the best idea but I'm telling her before he comes. I clear my throat.

"Hey mom?" I question, forcing myself to stop shaking my leg.

A habit I had when I was nervous. I knew she would know something is up right away.

"So as you know, I have been seeing an older guy..." I trail, Aiden wasn't that much older than I, only about a seven-year difference.

She at-least knew he was twenty-seven and understood

because she and my dad shared the same gap in years and also met at the same age as Aiden and I.

I hoped she would be understanding.

"He's my professor." I blurt out and I watch as her features twist.

"Journie! Are you sure this is the best idea?" She asks, looking at me concerned.

"You do know that can come with major consequences and conflict with your education, don't you?"

She asks, getting up from her seat. I also get up from mine, running a hand through my hair.

"Yes." I say, my mom always told me I was wise beyond my years. I doubted that in this very moment.

"I trust your judgment, honey, but you really shouldn't be having that kind of relationship while he is still your professor." I nod my head. I already knew this.

"We bought fought it for a while, mom. I didn't instantly jump at him, we tried to keep our distance, as much as we could. But fate had other plans and we would always end up together, somehow. He was the one who helped me fix my car the very first day I moved here." I say and I watch her mouth fall open.

"That explains it." She simply says and walks over to pull me into a hug.

"You felt protected by him because he was the first one you met here. Of course, there is some sort of bond there." She realizes, pulling away from me.

"I thought you had only met in class and started forming a relationship there."

"No, I doubt it would have happened if those were the circumstances." She takes a sip of her coffee,
"I can't say I approve, Journie. You are going to have to be careful these next few months. You both are legal adults so really, I don't see much they could do, but for your education and well-being. I think it's best if you keep it to a minimum while he's still your professor. That means you absolutely cannot have any kind of contact with him other than things related to class on campus." I scratch my head at that, my mind reeling back to last week.
My cheeks instantly felt flustered, and I knew by the look she was giving me she already knew.
"Journie, he hasn't touched you, has he?" She asked, concerned. I shake my head rapidly, and he hasn't. Not in that way yet.
Sure, we've gotten hot and heavy during make out sessions but that was it. I wanted to go further, but I knew in my rationalized mind that wasn't the best idea. At least not yet.
"No. We have had heavy make out sessions but nothing beyond that." I confess. She nods.
"Keep it that way, at-least until you aren't in his class anymore." I didn't respond and about that time, a knock came at my door. My heart rate instantly sped up, it was now or never.
I told Aiden prior to him coming that I would be telling my mom and he agreed that it would be the best idea. I swing the door open and see him standing there with two bouquet of flowers. A smile instantly appears on my face as I let him in. My mom loved flowers, that kiss up.

Could you blame him though?

"Mrs. Derringer, how lovely to meet you." Aiden says, handing her a bouquet of flowers. I could see the crack in my mom's hard exterior and smirked. She was just as smitten with him as I was.

"These are beautiful! Thank you so much!" She exclaims, placing them in a vase of water.

"And for you, my beautiful lady." He turned to me, handing me the other bouquet. Except mine had a note I couldn't wait to read.

"Aiden!" I squeal, placing them on the table and tackling him with a hug. He was a keeper, and I didn't care how long and twisted our road got, I was in for the ride, for the unseeable future.

He placed a light kiss on my forehead, leaning down to whisper in my ear.

"I take it she wasn't too shocked?" I shook my head.

"She had her suspicions and reacted exactly how I expected her too." I say and pull away from her. My mom cleared her throat and we both turn to look at her.

"I can't say that I approve at this moment, but I'm also not going to tell you, that you can't be together. Journie, I support you and I love you, no matter what. And Aiden..." she trailed, looking him dead in the eyes.

"I trust that you will take care of her and treat her right. And I thank you for being there for my baby." She smiles, turning around to fix our plates. I made lasagna, one of my favorite dishes. I let out a long breath I didn't realize I was holding and made a mental note to ask Aiden about his family later.

He hasn't really mentioned them all that much and I could only assume he wasn't that close to them.

As I took a seat next to him, I could feel the heat radiating off his body.

I wanted nothing more than to kiss him and have him against me. I feel a hand squeeze my thigh and a shiver runs down my spine. It was good to know he felt the same. As soon as my mother left, my lips would be on his.

ELEVEN:

AIDEN

Once I arrived back at my house that night, Journie was on my mind more than usual. I opened my cabinet and twisted the lid to a bottle of liquor. If I weren't careful, I could fall back into my old patterns, and I did not want her to see that side of me.

I took a sip, placing it back down on the counter. I had some serious thinking to do. I knew from the moment I met her; she was something special.

I knew she wouldn't be my student for much longer, but I knew she still had at least a good three years left to finish her degree. Even after she finished my class, we would still have to be careful. There was always the option of me finding somewhere else to teach, but I really did love teaching at NYU.

I knew the better option would for me to find another job, I didn't want her to have to give up going here for me.

I knew she would try to put up a fight and argue that we could keep it on the down low but even right now it was hard to keep my hands off her. I had only a few rules and I have broken every single one of them in a matter of weeks.

I take another sip, welcoming the burn. I felt dirty, feeling this way about a student. I was supposed to be the one she looked up to, the one to teach her, the one to guide her when she was needing help, and all on a professional level.

I had never been an open book, until she waltzed into my life. I felt the need to tell her about my past, which I haven't done yet, but would soon. She told me about her parents and now it was only fair she knew about mine. I didn't have the best childhood and seeing as I was the only child, I should have had it better.

I felt like I was turning her life upside down and I didn't want to be the cause of any mental problems for her. I needed to talk to her and as each day drug on, the urge got stronger.

I knew it was overwhelming for her to move to an unfamiliar place and almost immediately start a taboo relationship with her professor.

I was grateful her mom understood, although she didn't quite approve, I had it in my best interest to change that. Having her mom's approval meant everything to me.

I would even quit my job teaching if I had to prove that Journie and I had the same rights as every other couple. It could have been worse. My phone buzzed beside me, bringing me back to reality.

-What's up? -J

I smile, thinking of a reply.

-Thinking of you, as always. What're you up to? -A

My phone buzzed within seconds; a picture appeared on my screen.

My heart began beating faster, and I could feel my body heat up. I wanted her here with me more than anything. I wanted her to sleep next to me at night, I wanted to have her near at every waking moment. I analyzed the picture, smiling.

She was lying in her bed, hair pulled on top of her head and a cute pair of glasses framed her face. Her favorite book in her hands and I could spot a cup of coffee on her bedside table.

-Beautiful, as always. I wish you were here. -A

-On my way. -J

It takes a moment to register in my buzzed state that she meant she was coming over. It was late on a Friday night, and I really didn't want her out driving alone. I was obviously not able to, so I guess I would have to suck it up. I racked my brain for her favorite movie and rushed over to my TV.

I knew she would be into a sappy romance decided to just let her pick when she arrived.

I placed the liquor bottle back into the cabinet and drank some water. I didn't even want her to see me in a buzzed state. I knew it would break her heart. I start a pot of fresh coffee,

I wanted her to be as comfortable as possible. I imagined she would be staying the night seeing as it was already eleven p.m.

An alien feeling bubbled inside of me, was it butterflies? I can't say I've ever had them before. No other woman has caught my eye like she has. A knock came at my door, and I ran over to it.

My heart pounded in my chest as I took in her appearance, her hair was still on top of her head, and the glasses still on her face. I immediately bring her to my chest and crash my lips to hers. Sweet, sweet innocence.

She pulled away all too soon, moving beside me to go in. "As fun as that was, it's a bit chilly out there." She giggles, walking over to my couch. I watch as her perfect figure takes a seat and brings her knees to her chest. I could tell something was on her mind, but I didn't want to bother her with it. I wanted her to come to me.

I take a seat beside her, pulling her into my chest. She lets out a big sigh and I lean down to kiss her forehead. I had to ask.

"Is everything okay, baby?" She slowly nods her head, but I have known her long enough to know when something was bothering her.

"Want to tell me what's really on your mind?" She moved her head to look at me, her deep eyes staring into mine.

"After you left, my mom told me she was also in a relationship. She hasn't really seen many men since my dad, and I don't know how to feel about it.

I want to be happy for her, because with any other circumstances she would have stayed with me tonight, but she said she needed to get back to him. I was okay with that but I'm not comfortable knowing she's with some random guy that I don't know anything about." She rants, as I keep my eyes on hers. She was missing the irony in her statement.

"Isn't that exactly how she should be feeling about you?"

I question as realization takes over her features. She bites down on her lip, deep in thought.
"It's different. She knows you."
"She only first met me today." I reason, but I get where she is coming from.
"Yeah, but she has known about our relationship basically since we started, and I have sent her pictures of you." She admits and I laugh.
"Baby, pictures and actually meeting the person aren't the same thing. All I'm saying is look at it from her point of view."
She huffed,
"I'm trying my best. At least I know she made it back safe."
"Do you want some coffee?" I ask, deciding I would tell her about my past another night, I didn't want to add onto her worries.
"The answer will always be yes." She beamed, getting up and placing a kiss on my lips but it wasn't enough for me. As she turned around, I grabbed her hand, pulling her onto my lap.
She smirked as she straddled me, placing soft kisses on my neck. I couldn't get enough of her, I wanted to consume all of her fire.
"Journie..." I trailed, bringing my hand up to take her hair down. It fell in soft waves around her face, and it lit me up inside. I lifted her head with my hand and cupped the sides of her face. I stared into her eyes, my heart pounding.
"Do you have any idea how beautiful you are?"

I whisper, not giving her enough time to respond before pressing my lips to hers for the hundredth time. She pressed herself onto me harder and suddenly I didn't want coffee anymore. I wanted every inch of her.
I wanted to make every part of her body mine. I knew I couldn't have it all just yet so for now, this would have to suffice. I pressed my hips into hers, earning a moan from her lips. It was my second favorite sound on the earth, the first being her laugh.
Every sound she made was like music to my ears. I moved my hands to lay her down, so I was hovering over her. My hands found the bottom of her shirt and she lifted her arms above her head. I loved how eager she was.
I peeled it off her, throwing her shirt on the floor. I took in the sight before me and groaned. I needed her. All of her.
"So beautiful." I say and take my own shirt off. I take her in my arms and press our bodies closer together.
She wraps her legs around my waist, pushing herself against me. I'm not sure how much more I can take without breaking.
"Please don't stop." She whimpered, looking into my eyes. How could I when she was looking at me like that? I didn't want too, but I knew I had to. For both of our sakes. I break away from her neck, looking apologetically in her eyes.
"Baby, we can't not yet." I say and caress her cheek. She nods her head and I smirk.
"But that doesn't mean we can't do other things," I continue, giving her a wide grin.

"Is this okay?" I ask, making sure before we went any further. She nods, squirming beneath me.
"Good," I breathe, reaching my hands up to unhook her bra.
"Because I want to taste you." She gasps at that, moving to cover herself.
"You don't ever have to hide from me." I say as I place another soft kiss to her lips. She nods, breathing heavily.
"Are you ready?" I ask, trailing kisses down her stomach. I stopped right before I got to her most intimate part and I didn't even have to ask to know that she was.

TWELVE:

JOURNIE

I hear light snoring in my ear and jump up, quickly realizing I was in Aiden's bed. I lay back down as he wraps his strong arms around me, and I melt into them. Last night was like a dream and if going all the way felt better than that then I absolutely couldn't wait.

He was the man of my dreams, and I didn't want to waste any time in pursuing him. I turned over to check the time on my phone seeing it was close to eight. I quietly got up, throwing on one of his oversized t-shirts. I would be keeping it, that was for certain. It smelled just like him and I couldn't get enough.

I go into his kitchen and begin finding ingredients to make breakfast. I loved to cook and if it were for him, I loved it even more. I took my AirPods from my bag and plugged them in my ears.

Music was my go-to when I had a lot on my mind. And I had a ton. I wanted to know more about Aiden's past.

I didn't want to seem demanding, but I found it to be fair since he knew a lot about mine. I wanted to know everything there was to know about that man.

"Now that's a sight I love to see." Warm arms snake

around my waist, making me jump.
"Aiden! You are going to make me drop the eggs." I scold, placing them gently down on the counter.
"Need any help?" He asks, placing a light kiss on my forehead.
"Nope. Enjoy your coffee." I say as he pours a cup.
"How do you like yours?" He asks, grabbing another cup from the cabinet.
"Three cream and four sugar." I liked mine sweet and mostly cold, but I was feeling rather warm today.
"Same as me, good to know." He smiled, setting a cup beside me.
"Thanks babe." I say, standing on my tiptoes to kiss his cheek. This was something I could get used to, lazy Saturday mornings.
"Anything for you." He takes a seat at the table, picking up a newspaper to read. I let out a laugh. I didn't think people still done that.
"Why are you laughing?" He questions, raising an eyebrow at me.
"I didn't think people read those anymore." I shrug, placing the eggs onto a plate. I sucked at making bacon, so eggs and sausage were my go-to.
"I'm an old man at heart." I laugh again, he had a good sense of humor.
"I believe that one hundred percent." I smile and serve him his plate. He smiled at me and mumbled a small thank you before digging in.
I took the seat in-front of him, stuffing my face along with

Once we both finished, he got up and I followed.
"You cooked and now I get to clean." He says, taking a towel and throwing it over his shoulder. I let my eyes roam his muscles and wished he was in my arms. Selfish, I know.
"Go find a movie for us to watch." He says and nods over towards the tv.
"Ooh let's watch Happy Death Day!" I exclaim, taking my place on the couch. Memories of last night flood my mind and I instantly shiver. I could feel my cheeks heat up as I remembered how his tongue felt against me. I loved every second of it.
"That's not a sappy romance!" I hear Aiden say from the kitchen and I laugh.
"I don't always watch sappy things." I reply, laying back and pulling a blanket over me.
The next hour and a half were filled with much needed cuddling and kissing, and we did watch some of the movie.
Aiden was so distracting.
"Journie," He begins, lifting his head from my shoulder.
"Mhm?" I question.
"I need to talk to you." He says and my heart rate speeds up. Was he second guessing our relationship?
"I'm all ears." I say, sitting up and crossing my legs. I wanted to be fully aware.
"My past hasn't been so great. I wanted to open up to you like you have me." He says, taking sip of water. I could tell by the way he was twiddling his thumbs that he was nervous.

"I'm listening." I reiterate, taking his hands into mine. He was slightly shaking. I could tell this was a huge deal to him. His big blue eyes stared so deeply into mine and I couldn't help but get lost in them.

"I used to be an alcoholic. I got into it my early teen years because I had no parents that cared. I hung out with the wrong crowds, pursued the wrong women. I was in and out of people's houses until I was in college and could use a scholarship to afford to live on campus. My grades were the only good thing I could maintain." His shaking subsided and I lifted my hand to touch his cheek.

"Oh, Aiden. I'm so sorry." I say, trying to think of better words to say.

"I was the only child. I had no siblings to fuss with or to share my toys with. You would think it was perfect, but it wasn't." He blows out a breath, taking another sip of water. A tear escapes his eye and that's when I break.

He was so strong. He lifted his hand to wipe away my tears and it only caused me to bawl more. I was grateful for the man sitting before me. I was grateful that even though he had a terrible past that he was able to break free from it and become the man he is today.

"Baby don't cry." He whispers, placing his forehead against mine. I sniffle and suck it up. I felt so bad for him.

"You started it." I try to joke, and he cracks a smile.

"I am so glad I got away from those things, then I would have never met you." He smiled, placing a kiss on my lips.

"I don't even want to imagine how that would be." I say, resting my head on his shoulder.

"It would be a very colorless world." He kisses me with so much passion, I fear I'm going to spontaneously combust.

THIRTEEN

AIDEN

I watched as Journie sat on the edge of my desk, a book in her hand. She was supposed to be helping me sort files, but she was too cute reading. I couldn't bother her.

The light in my office was dim and there wasn't a single soul in the building. I could be doing so many other things with her at the moment, but I just wanted to enjoy her company.

Even if we weren't speaking any words to each other, there was a comfort I couldn't quite explain.

"Journie?" I ask, bringing her back to reality.

"Yeah?" She questioned, looking up from her book. She was the most beautiful person I had ever laid my eyes on.

"Do you want to go get something to eat? We can drive to the next city over and eat in? There is the really cool retro diner that I love." I babble and her eyes light up, I have been wanting to take her on a proper date and it was weighing on me that I couldn't.

"Yes!" She jumped up, throwing her book on the desk and jumping into my lap. I couldn't help the smile that formed on my face. I was falling deeply for her as the days went on. I was addicted to her, and I needed December to get here.

I place a gentle kiss on her lips. She tasted like sweet honey. She gets up from my lap and it takes everything in me to not pull her back and stay here. I stand up, offering her my jacket.

She happily obliges and I almost laugh as it swallows her. She looked so good in my clothing. October was upon us, and it was cool outside. It was my favorite time of year and now that I had Journie, it was even better.

"Ready?" I ask as I shut the lights off to my office and follow her out of the door. There were only a few good things that came out of staying later and that was everyone else had already gone home and it did earn a bit more privacy with Journie in a public place.

"Yes!" She answered again, climbing eagerly into my car. My chest swelled with the thought of how happy she was, I wanted to make her happy every day. It was my goal to make sure she was satisfied each waking day.

"Is that big enough for you?" I smirked at her, eyeing the huge burger in-front of her. She shrugged, taking a huge bite. She closed her eyes in delight, and I laughed.

"Its soo good." She mused, taking another bite. I had to admit, I didn't like burgers all that much but hers looked delicious. Not as delicious as her, though.

"I'm glad you are enjoying it." I say and take a bite of my chicken sandwich. It wasn't quite as grand as hers, but it was my favorite.

"This is nice." She compliments, reaching over the table to grab my hand. I almost jump away and realized we were the only people in here and relaxed.
"I can't wait until we can fully be with each other." I sigh, I wanted it as much as she did.
"Me too baby, me too." I lift her hand to my lips and kiss it softly. I wanted to have as much contact with her as possible.
Once we finish our meal, we head back to my place. I was ready for dessert. As much as I would like for it to be Journie, I baked a cheesecake last night for us to eat. She could still be part of the dessert though; I doubt she would mind.
Images of her squirming beneath me filled my mind and I knew she would be my first round. The cheesecake could wait.
As soon as we walked through my door, I was instantly on her. She kissed me back with so much passion and I couldn't wait to have full control over her.
I pressed her into the counter and wrapped her thigh around my waist. I wanted her so badly and I didn't know how much longer I could resist. I want to say screw the rules and just do it.
She pressed herself into me and I held onto her tighter. I bring my hands down to grip her bottom,
"Aiden..." She trailed, placing kisses down my neck.
"I want you." She whimpers, moving away for a second to stare into my eyes.
"Don't tempt me baby."

"I mean it." She says, unwrapping herself from me. She stands a few feet away from me and begins to take her shirt off.

"Are you sure?" I question, taking a step closer to her and taking her into my arms.

"Yes." She says, placing another kiss on my neck.

"Follow me." I say and lead her upstairs into my bedroom. I wanted to do it right. I knew she was still a virgin and I wanted to take care of her. Even though I didn't really need too, I shut the door and locked it behind us. My heart was pounding.

"Are you sure?" I ask again, I didn't want her to feel like I was taking advantage of her. Instead of answering me, she strips down to nothing, but her underwear and I knew then she meant it.

"Lay down." I say and she nods, climbing onto my bed. I took in every inch of her. I strip of everything but my bottoms and climb on top of her. I place a gentle kiss on her forehead and then on her lips.

Every inch of her was so soft. I work my way down her body, kissing the insides of her thighs and I could see that she was more than ready for me.

I loved seeing her from the angle. It meant more to me that I was the only one who had ever seen her this way. I take my hand and touch her gently, earning a groan of satisfaction from her.

"Please Aiden," She begs as I kiss her. Without delaying it any longer, I give her one last kiss on the lips before fully taking her.

FOURTEEN:

AIDEN

I stared down at the envelope in my hands. A shiver ran down my spine and I knew it wasn't from the cool October air that creeped through my open windows. The envelope wasn't labeled, and I wondered if I should open it. It was strange, I opened my door and almost slipped on it.

I still had another thirty minutes before class began and curiosity was getting to me. Once I sat down and got all my things situated, I opened the envelope.

Its contents immediately made my heart drop. Inside was a photo of Journie and I at the diner. We weren't doing anything but smiling at each other. It couldn't really be used as proof of a relationship but then I took the next picture out and my heart sank even more.

It was Journie and I kissing in my classroom. I knew it. I knew we should have been more careful but because I couldn't resist temptation, someone found out.

I throw the envelope on my desk and run a hand through my hair. A slip of paper hits the floor and I reach down to grab it.

'She's mine. Back off.'

I had to tell Journie. We absolutely had to keep our hands off each other at campus.

As hard as that was going to be. I wonder if it were one of my students. Surely it wasn't another professor.
But I could be very wrong. I do know Professor Gavin doesn't really like me, but I don't think he would be behind this. He tends to avoid me. I get up from my seat frustrated and I couldn't even tell Journie right away. It was killing me. I needed to go somewhere to think. I gathered my things and went to the office.
I let them know I was cancelling classes for the day and that I would be back tomorrow. Envelope in hand, I headed out to my car. I had a lot of investigating to do.
Moments later, my phone buzzed, and I knew it was Journie. I hadn't told her anything. I thought for a second before I replied.
-Hey baby, I'm not feeling all too well. I'm about to go home. -A
Seconds later, I receive a reply.
-On my way. -J
Right now really wasn't the best time for us to be together and if she also skipped the rest of her classes, that would raise even more flags.
Before I could register what was happening, my car door swung open and Journie climbed into the passenger seat.
I don't think I have ever hidden something so fast in my life. I needed to break it to her, but I didn't know how.
She narrowed her eyes at me.
"Do you want to tell me what's really going on?" I let out a loud sigh and handed her the envelope. It was now or never.

I watched her face as she pulled out the pictures and let out a gasp. She slowly turned to me, her eyes blazing. I watched as she examines the note and her eyes filled with tears.

"What do we do now?" I shrug my shoulders, backing out of the parking lot. I knew that I needed her, and I didn't want anything else in this moment.

We arrived at my place, there was a note taped to my door. I snatched it down and ushered Journie inside. I couldn't possibly think of anyone who could be sabotaging us like this.

Once inside I threw the envelope down on my couch not bothering to open it yet. I turned to Journie and pulled her into my arms. I buried my head into her neck. I never wanted anything to come between us, and as much as I didn't want to resign from my position, I knew it would have to come to that.

Now especially since someone knew and was blackmailing us. I removed my head from her neck and placed a soft kiss on her forehead.

"I'll resign." I say simply, as if it would solve all our problems. I knew it wouldn't, but it was nice to think that it could.

"Aiden, no. I'm sure I could transfer to another university. That's your job." She says exactly what I thought she would.

"No. I would rather find somewhere else to teach." I argue back and she rolls her eyes.

"I'm not letting you give up something you love." She says and I shrug.

"I wouldn't be." I say, looking at her intently. Those three words bounced around in my head and it hit me like a freight train.
I was in-love with Journie and would follow her to the ends of the earth if I had too.
"We'll just have to be cautious. Obviously, this person knows where I live, so even you being here at the moment is a risk." I say and move a strand of hair that had fallen off into her face.
"It shouldn't be this way." She huffs, taking a seat on my couch.
"A teacher should never fall for a student, but here we are." I say and sit beside her. I picked up the envelope and opened it carefully. I was surprised whoever done this, would take it as far as my house.
At that point, it could be considered trespassing but to even do anything about it, Journie and I would have to reveal our relationship. I doubt anyone could be after her, she hadn't been here long enough for anyone to feel this way about her. Unless she knew something I didn't.
"Baby?" I question and she looks over at me. Instead of answering, she raises and eyebrow at me.
"Do you know of anyone who could be behind this?" Her gaze avoided mine and I knew there was something she didn't want to tell me.
"Journie baby, you have to tell me."
She heaved a loud sigh and turned to fully look at me.
"This may be a long shot, but my junior year of high school, there was this boy who was stalking me. I mean

like showing up to my house and looking through my window and sneaking pictures of me.
He would threaten me at school. I finally got the courage to tell my mom and we got a restraining order against him, and he then eventually moved..." She trailed, and my anger was blazing. I knew Journie was beautiful, anyone with sight could see that.
I wanted to find him and kill him for how he treated her. A woman like Journie should be cherished and not taken advantage of.
"You think it could be him?" I question, and she nods, a tear falling from her eye.
"It's the exact same method that he used. No doubt." I pulled her onto my lap and wiped away her tears. I placed a kiss on her forehead and then on her cheek.
"What does he look like? What's his name?" I question, I needed to put a face and I really needed a name so I could look more into him.
"He's got brown hair, kind of like yours. Last time I saw him it was short, then again that was a few years ago. He's got blue eyes and he's a little bit shorter than you. His name is Andrew." She speaks and I take all of it in.
"It will be okay. It's risky but I think you should stay here with me. I'll resign and we can go to the police. I don't think there are strong rules against student professor relationships, but I will ask." I say, if they can't prove anything sexual has been going on, then we should be okay. Unless that bastard has a photo.
I pull Journie closer to me, making sure to soak up every

moment with her.

"I like that idea." She says, burying her head into my chest. I take a deep breath and those three words are in my mind again, I want to tell her but not this way. Not yet. I wanted to make that moment special.

FIFTEEN:

JOURNIE

Two pink vibrant lines. The image was etched into my head. I tried to shake it away, but it wouldn't leave. It was a permanent mark. My hands were shaking as I sat in the floor of Aiden's bathroom.

How would he take it? Would he make me leave? I shoved the test back into the box and placed it back into my purse. It had only been a few weeks since we first done the deed, so that means I would have conceived on our very first night together. I didn't know when or how to tell him. I was only nineteen, about to turn twenty and I still had my whole college career ahead of me. I know it would be extremely difficult with a baby.

Only a few days had passed since we got the envelope and I have been trying to stay as close to Aiden as possible. I decided to stay at home today because I wasn't feeling too well and now, I know the reason.

Aiden and I have been trying to keep as discreet as possible. I knew we weren't in the clear just yet and our relationship was still in jeopardy. I knew any minute he could text me and say that he's resigned, or he's been called to talk to the Dean. I curl up on the couch and put

Netflix on, wanting to take my mind off things.

"Baby?" I hear in my ear and jolt up.
"Are you hungry?" His soft voice fills my ears, and I can feel my cheeks heat up at how close he is to me.
"Starving." I reply and get up. The events from earlier filled my head and suddenly I felt so nauseous.
"Takeout?" He questioned and I nod. Despite feeling nauseous, Chinese sounded amazing.
"Chinese! I want Lo-Mein and Fried Shrimp."
"Weird combo but okay." He laughs and places a kiss on my cheek. I adored that his love language was affection. I soaked it up.
I guess in a way mine was too, whenever he was near, I had to be having some sort of physical contact with him. I don't think I would ever grow tired of him.
He was my safe place and I needed that now more than ever. A chill ran down my spine thinking about that. I had to be extra careful when I went out in public, and Aiden didn't really like for me to go alone. But seeing as it was extremely difficult for us to go out in public together, we resulted to groceries being delivered or just him going out to get them.
I excuse myself to the bathroom and look at myself in the mirror. My long blond locks were thrown in a messy bun and one of Aiden's sweatshirts hung loosely on me.
I turned to my side and place a hand on my stomach. I knew I couldn't be more than a few weeks. It was the

middle of October and Halloween was coming up. Thoughts of a Halloween surprise ran through my head, and I knew then that was what I wanted to do. Given that he didn't catch on before then. I was getting sick in the mornings and had missed my period.

I lift my shirt up and examine my stomach. I didn't even know if Aiden wanted any kids, but something tells me that he would be thrilled.

We hadn't known each other but for a few months but I knew he was the one for me. There was just something about him and the way he treated me was like gold.

I put my shirt back down and go back into the kitchen a steaming cup of coffee waiting for me.

He already knew me like the back of my hand.

"Thank you." I muse, leaning up to kiss him on the cheek.

"Anything for you baby. Are you feeling any better?" He asks, taking the seat Infront of me.

"Much better now that you are here." I say and take a sip. I knew I wouldn't be able to enjoy as much caffeine now and I wanted to soak up all that I could.

Aiden's phone dings and almost makes me jump.

"Foods here!" He exclaims running to open the front door. To make Aiden happy all you had to really do was feed him. A smile spread across my face as I watch him grab the food and happily trot over to the kitchen table.

"Dig in baby!"

I oblige with no second thoughts, mixing all my food together. Aiden gives me some weird looks, but I ignore them. It was delicious. I offer my bowl towards him.

"Want a bite?" I question, shoveling another bite into my mouth.
"All yours." He twists his face in disgust and I laugh.
"Suit yourself." I say as I finish it off. I lean back in my chair and rub my stomach. I close my eyes to relax, but then the wave of nausea hit me.
I rush up from my chair and run into the bathroom. Aiden is immediately behind me, making sure that I am okay.
"Eat to fast?" He asks as I nod my head.
"I knew it wasn't a good combo." He shrugs and I glare at him. He holds his hands up in surrender.
"Kidding. Kidding." He smiles and pulls me into his chest. My favorite place to be. I take deep breaths to try and settle my stomach.
Next thing I know, I am being lifted from the ground and held in Aiden's arms.
"Let's go to bed. You need some rest." He whispers, placing a soft kiss on my forehead. I can only manage a small nod.
Once we get to our bedroom, I take off his sweatshirt, leaving me only in my undergarments. Most nights I slept with only his t-shirt, but I was feeling too hot for that.
"T-shirt?" He questions and I shake my head.
"I'm going to go take a quick shower before we lay down." I say and lean up to kiss his cheek.
"Do that and I'll clean. I expect big cuddles when you get out." He smirks and slaps my butt as I walk into the bathroom. I toss my hair over my shoulder and wink at him.

"We'll see."

SIXTEEN:

JOURNIE

My fingers drummed on my thigh as I listened to Aiden. I was ready for his class to be over so that way I could eat. I hadn't had breakfast yet, due to me being nauseous but right now I felt like I could eat a buffet. I wanted all the Sausage, Bacon and Eggs I could get.

I held on to my stomach as it rumbled and got up from my chair. I couldn't wait any longer. I tossed Aiden a look before leaving, mumbling a quick sorry. I knew a moment later he would text me and I would tell him then. I made my way over to the Café.

Once I fixed my plate, I felt my phone buzz in my pocket and knew immediately who it was from.

-Are you okay? - A

-Yes, I was hungry. -J

-Typical. I hope you know you missed a good lecture. -A

-You can give it to me later ;)-J

-Don't say things like that while I'm in teacher mode, you don't want to know the things I'd do to you right now. -A

I couldn't help but laugh, knowing I looked crazy to anyone else who might be looking. I put my phone down and continued eating.

"Well, well who do we have here?" A chill ran down my spine. It couldn't be. Could it? I chose to ignore him. I could feel my heart begin to race and fear strike through me.

"Cat got your tongue?" I shook my head, not daring to look up at him.

"Professor Bennett have you that much on a tight rope?"

"Shut up!" I growl, getting up from my seat. I look him dead in the eyes, adrenaline filling my veins.

"I have a restraining order against you. I am not afraid to call the police!" I bark, picking up my tray.

"And then what? I'll expose your relationship with your precious Mr. Bennett, and he will be right there with me."

I bite down on my lip, choosing my next words carefully.

"Leave me alone!" I shout, hoping someone would notice the discomfort I was in. Andrew takes a step towards me and I shuffle backward, almost tripping over my feet.

"Please." I beg, tears threatening to spill over. I didn't want to cause too much of a scene.

He was violating the restraining order just by being this close.

"Take one more step and I'll call the police." I say and pull my phone from my pocket.

"I have evidence, sexual evidence of you being with him. There's nothing you can do if you want to keep your relationship with him!" He shouts and takes another step towards me. At this point I was visibly shaking, and I knew I had to get out. The only instinct I had was to lift my hand up and slap him.

He stumbled backward, keeping his hand on his face.
"You whore! Just wait!" He shouts as I run out of the cafe.
I don't think I have ever run so fast in my life. I ran towards the nearest bathroom and threw everything I just ate up. I sat in the floor with my hands over the toilet and as disgusting as it was, I felt relief. I had to tell Aiden. I had to tell him that I had just run into Andrew.

Once I was done, I cleaned up the best I could and walked towards his classroom. I knew it wasn't the best idea but right now I just needed him. I don't care who was around.
I knock on his door lightly and his gaze shoots up to me. He stands up quickly and ushers me in. Thankfully he was on a break in between classes.

"Baby are you okay?" He questions, pulling me close to him. I shake my head rapidly. I couldn't help the tears that escaped my eyes.

"H-he's here. He talked to me. He threatened me." I spill out into his chest, and I immediately feel him tense.

"Where is he now?" I shook my head.

"I don't know." I say and look up at him. His cheeks were a crimson red.

"You have to tell the Dean." He says and I shake my head again.

"I can't. He said he has evidence of us sexually being together. Now whether or not that is true." I trail off, looking into his deep eyes. He sighs.

"I'll go put my notice in. Your safety is much more important to me. I can find somewhere else to teach." This time, I didn't even argue.

"Okay." I whisper as he hands me a set of keys.

"Go and stay in my office. Lock the door behind you, you'll be safe there." He leans down and places a kiss on my forehead and wipes the tears from my face.

I'll never understand what I did to deserve someone like him.

I walk into his office and make sure to lock the door behind me. I lay down on the couch and cover with a blanket, hoping a nap would take my mind off things.

Maybe once Aiden resigned, we could be happy together, but I knew deep down that it wouldn't. Not for a while.

A loud knock on the door awakens me and I jolt up. The familiarity of Aiden's office overwhelms me, and I realize where I am.

I jump up and throw the blanket off me. I look through the peephole before opening it, revealing a tired-looking Aiden.

"Let's go home baby. I have until this weekend to get all my things. They were surprised but understood. I told them that due to personal reasons, I wouldn't be able to teach at the university anymore." I nod my head and grab my purse. I toss it over my shoulder and realize the pregnancy test is still in there. I needed to tell Aiden. I had to tell him. Sooner than Halloween. I follow Aiden out into the empty hallway, knowing this was probably also my last time walking the halls with him. It was too late in the semester to drop my classes so, unfortunately;

I would have to finish them out here.
On the way back home, I made a mental note to call my mom. I needed to update her on the situation. She wouldn't be thrilled to know he found out where I was.
Moments after we walk into the door, I sit on the couch and dial my mom's number. She picks up on the third ring. "Hey sweetie, how are you?" I take a deep breath and she immediately knows something is up.
"Tell me Journie."
"He's back." I manage out, taking deep breaths to calm my heart rate.
"Who is baby?" Aiden's strong arms wrap around me as I stand up. I lean into him.
"Andrew, mom. He found me at school today and threatened to expose Aiden and I's relationship." I could hear her gasp on the other end of the phone.
"Are you okay honey? You need to call the police." She speaks. Tears fall from my eyes for the millionth time today.
"I can't mom. He has evidence that Aiden and I are in a relationship. I can't do anything until the end of the semester. Aiden resigned today but that doesn't mean we are in the clear." I sob as Aiden's grip tightens on me.
"Stay as close to him as possible."
"I will as much as I can."
"Keep me updated. I love you."
"I love you too." I say and end the call. I loved my mom to death and it meant a lot to me that she thought Aiden could take care of me.

"I'll run you a hot bath?" Aiden suggests and I nod my head. That sounded like exactly what I needed right now.
"Glass of wine?" I shake my head. Definitely not.
"Go grab some clothes and I'll run it for you." I nod my head and make my way up the stairs. Could he be any more perfect? A feeling of pure love waved over me. Was this what it felt like to be in love? Aiden was the perfect man for me.
I push open the bathroom door to see he has lit a few candles and has my favorite songs playing quietly in the background.
"What do you want to eat?"
"Spaghetti sounds great." He leans down to kiss my forehead.
"Anything for you baby." A wide smile spreads across my face.
"And desserts going to be a personal favorite of mine." He winks and slaps my butt as I undress. I couldn't wait.

SEVENTEEN

JOURNIE

Staring down at my books, I sigh loudly. It wasn't anywhere near as entertaining here without Aiden. I missed having him in lectures and being able to stare at him.

It had only been a week since he resigned and was looking for another teaching job. He was looking at some of the community colleges here in New York.

He wouldn't be able to start until January anyways. If I needed to, I could always get a job to help. I need to start saving for the baby.

Speaking of Halloween was next week and I couldn't wait to tell him. I had taken several more tests and all of them were positive. I kept one for the reveal. I hoped he didn't get mad at me for waiting so long.

I'd already set up an appointment for November the first. I was stoked. I hoped Aiden would be too.

I closed my books and took a moment to relax. I had another thirty minutes before my next class began. Thankfully I hadn't had any more run-ins with Andrew, but I felt like that would be short-lived. I always made sure to check my surroundings and tried to never be alone.

Thankfully the library was always busy about this time of day. Looking at my watch I realized it's almost time for my last class of the day to start and jump up. I hurriedly grab my books and shove them into my bag.
"Where are you going beautiful?" All the hair on my body stands up straight and my veins run cold. I try to ignore him but it's no use. He's practically yelling. I put my head down and call Aiden. He thankfully picks up on the first ring.
"Hey baby is everything alright?" His smooth voice instantly calms me.
"I-I" I stammer, trying to find the right words. I make my way into the bathroom, making sure to lock the door behind me.
"Journie, answer me."
"I don't want to be here anymore. I don't think I can finish the semester."
"What happened?" I take a deep breath.
"Andrew." I sputter out. I wanted to try my best to stay and finish the semester and I knew on campus there wasn't much Andrew could do because of the restraining order and because it was a public place but even just seeing him was too much.
Especially if he were going to confront me like that. If I didn't finish the semester here, then we could go to the police. It sounded like the best idea at this time.
"I'm coming to get you, baby. Stay where you are until I get there. I'll stay on the phone with you." I nod my head and realize he couldn't see me.

I wipe at the tears that fell from my eyes. I knew I still had many years ahead of me to get my degree but right now there were more important things I had to worry about.

I hoped by the time January rolled around all of this would be sorted out. I wanted to be with Aiden with no complications.

It took Aiden no time to reach campus and once he did, I sprinted out to his car like a track star. Once settled into the car, I could feel the nausea roll over me. I was ready to get this morning sickness over with.

Thankfully it didn't happen much, but when it did, I was done for. I swing open the car door before he has the chance to pull off and spill the contents of my stomach onto the pavement. I hear Aiden's door open, and he is immediately by my side.

He squats down and moves my hair away from my face. I didn't know how I got so lucky. It was extremely hard keeping this from him.

"Are you okay?" He asks and I manage a weak nod.

"Yes. I think I just got worked up from running so fast. Can we go home and cuddle?" I ask and wipe my face with a napkin. He leans up and places a kiss on my forehead.

"Your wish is my command." If it were even possible my love for Aiden grew a thousand times more.

Aiden's lips trailed down my neck as I swatted his hand away from my bottom.

"We're supposed to be cuddling." I giggle and turn towards him.
"You know there's not much cuddling when I'm in the room." He winks and I feel the heat rising to my face. He continues to place small kisses along my neck, and I can't help the moan that escapes my lips.
Today was perfect, we've been lazy, and it was the best distraction.
He lightly pushes me over onto my back and hovers over me. He leans down and presses his lips to mine softly, but that wasn't enough for me.
I grip the back of his neck and pull his body fully onto mine, feeling him against me.
He places his knee in between my thighs, pulling them apart. I wrap them around his waist and pull away from his lips to trail kisses down his neck. He lets out a low moan and I smirk. It was one of my favorite sounds.
"You are such a tease." He lowers his head to my neck, breathing heavily. I feel his hands under my shirt, the cool touch of them sending chills down my spine. I arch my back as he begins rocking back and forth.
"Who's the tease again?" I say, my lips reconnecting with his as his fingers find my waistband.
He slowly removes my pants while trailing kisses down my stomach.
"Do you think it's ok to have dessert before the main course?" His breath is hot on my thigh. The only thing I can do is swallow hard and nod. I am aching for his touch. His fingers brush lightly over my most sensitive spot and I shiver at his soft touch.

"I thought so too." He whispers, fulfilling my ache.
My hands immediately go to his hair, lightly pulling on it. The moan from his lips vibrates me, almost bringing me to the edge. He suddenly stops and I am cold from the absence of his lips.
"I need you now." He groans. He doesn't waste a second in filling me completely. He nuzzles his head into my neck, his teeth lightly graze my ear.
"I love you." He whispers, pulling away to stare deep into my eyes. I bring my lips to his.
"I love you." I reply, a single tear escaping my eye. I meant it, too.
I never knew I could love someone this much. I knew then at that moment he would be more than happy to start a family with me.
I had to bite my lip to keep from telling him. He was my perfect man, and I couldn't wait to start our future.

EIGHTEEN

AIDEN

Journie threw her arms around my neck, clinging to me. It was a feeling I would never get enough of. The love I had for her was nothing like anything I have ever experienced before. From the moment I met her, I just knew.

Her hot breath tickled my neck, bringing me back to reality. A shiver ran through me as her soft lips placed a kiss at the base of my neck. I closed my eyes. She knew *exactly* how to please me.

"Baby," I begin, looking at our surroundings. I took her to the diner; it had become our favorite place to eat. Technically we didn't have to hide anymore, but I still wanted to play it safe in public.

"No one's out here." She whispered, her own eyes scanning the parking lot. I held her tightly against me.

I place my finger under her chin and bring my lips to hers. She brought her hands up and lightly played with my hair, a moan escaping my lips. I pulled away for a moment,

"I love you." Leaves my lips as I place a kiss on her forehead. Her smile would be the death of me.

"And I love you." She replies, burying her head into my neck. I press her into the side of my car, tilting her head up

her head up for another kiss. Her lips were addicting. We really needed to get home before I take her right here.
"Journie baby we need to get home. Or else I'll take you right here." I whisper, moving a strand of hair from her face. She smirks at me, and I almost fall apart. The control this woman had over me was enticing.
She huffed and a pout settled on her lips. I couldn't help the smile that appeared on my face. I lean down to place one last kiss on her lips before taking her hand in mine and opening the door for her.
"Such a gentleman." She giggled, tossing me a seductive look before climbing in.

"Aiden." I turn my attention towards Journie, raising my eyebrows at her.
"I want to go home." She says simply, taking a sip of her coffee.
"You are home baby." I say and walk over to her.
"No, I mean I want to go home for the weekend. There are some things I need to tell my mom." She chewed on her bottom lip; her green eyes boring into mine.
"I think that's a great idea. When do you want to leave?"
"Tomorrow?" She questioned, her eyes hopeful.
"That's okay with me baby. I'd love to see where you grew up." She ran over to me, throwing her arms around my neck.
"You're the best." She smiles, kissing my cheek. I wanted her to be touching me, all the time.

Some would say I'm whipped but I'd just say I'm in love. Completely.

My phone buzzed in my pocket; I pull it out to see a missed call from the university. My heart drops. I swipe my phone open and click on the missed call, the phone immediately rings.

"Mr. Pickens speaking, how may I help you?" My heart is racing.

"It's Professor Bennett." I say,

"Professor Bennett! Just the person I was needing to speak with."

"Is everything alright?" I question, looking over at Journie who was sitting comfortably on the couch.

"Yes, yes. I was just wondering if you had time to come in and speak to me?

There are some things we need to discuss."

I glanced over at the clock, it was only five-thirty and I knew no one would be there.

"Sure. I'll be there in ten." I say and grab my keys. My heart was pounding. Did they know? They didn't ask for or about Journie, which was a good sign.

"Baby, the dean just called me and said he had some things to discuss. Do you feel safe staying here by yourself?" Her eyes widen.

"Do you think they know?" She questions, standing to her feet. I shrug.

"I don't think so, even if they did, they don't have solid evidence unless they see the picture of us kissing in my classroom."

I watch as her face twists in anger.
"I don't think Andrew would actually go that far."
"I do." I say as I kiss her forehead before walking out of the door.
After finding the envelope on my door, I had a good security camera and system installed so that way I could check on Journie when I wasn't around.
Occasionally I would have to leave her here by herself and I hated that.
Once I arrive at campus, I feel as if I might throw up from all the nerves. Once inside, I knocked on the door blowing out a large breath.
"Professor Bennett! Come on in." Mr. Pickens smiles at me and my nerves instantly settle. He doesn't know and if he does, it doesn't bother him
"Have a seat." I sit and cross my legs, to keep from shaking them.
"I brought you in here for you to reconsider. We are short-staffed now, and I have really good remarks on you. I want you to come back, Professor Bennett." When I didn't respond for a moment, he took a breath and continued,
"Of course, we would increase your pay." I thought about it. Journie wouldn't be a student here anymore, so I don't see a problem with working here. I took a deep breath, "Give me the weekend to consider and I will let you know on Monday." He nods his head and gives a light smile."Thank you for your time." I nod at him and stand up. I was relieved he didn't seem like he knew anything. Now, I just had to speak to Journie.

I rush home and find Journie knocked out on the couch. I noticed that she had been tired more than usual lately.

I knew she was under a lot of stress. If I could take it all away from her, I would in a heartbeat.

I lean down and kiss her forehead, awakening her. She gave me a groggy look and sat up when she realized it was me.

"How much trouble are we in?" She questions, bringing her knees to her chest. I sit beside her.

"None. They offered for me to come back, but I told him I would think about it. Now that you aren't a student there anymore, we could be together freely. If Andrew does submit those pictures to the university, they don't have a time stamp. There is no way of proving that we were together while you were a student there."

"And that means if he tries to sabotage us again, we can go to the police." She jumps into my lap and hugs my neck. I breathe in deep, taking in her sweet scent.

She always smelt like sweet honey. Maybe we could finally have a stress-free relationship. I wanted Journie to be in my life forever, no doubt. I pictured making her my wife and having kids together. She was my perfect woman.

NINETEEN

JOURNIE

A light kiss on my cheek woke me from my slumber. I don't think I would ever get used to him waking me up this way. I stretch my arms and groan. I could have used a little bit more time to sleep.

"Are you ready to eat breakfast?" He whispers in my ear and reaches his hand out to me. I groan again and take his hand. This was the first morning in a while that I haven't felt sick. I hoped it was subsiding. Thankfully Aiden was always asleep when it hit so he never heard me, that man could sleep through a tornado.

I was so excited to tell him on Halloween, I had the best announcement picked out. I wanted to tell my mom in person, and it was a good excuse to go home. I knew I needed to tell her more about Andrew but even just thinking about it makes me sick.

I fall into Aiden's arms, and he cradles me. I lived for these moments. Starting a family with him sounded perfect, I could already tell he was going to be the best father. My heart pounded at the thought of that, and I couldn't help the goofy grin that spread across my face. I had only known Aiden for a few short months, but I knew

hat I loved this man more than anything. He was my safe place, my comfort. I trusted him with my entire life.
"What do you want for breakfast baby?" I pull away from him and kiss his full lips.
"You." I say and trail my finger down his torso. He groans, bringing his hands down to grab my bottom. He gives a light squeeze and brings his hands to cup both sides of my face. My hormones are running wild. He stares deep into my eyes.
They are extra blue today, sparkling in the light. I always get lost in the depth of them. I could see everything he wanted to say in them. He leans down to whisper in my ear,
"Your wish is my command." He lightly bites my earlobe and lays me back down on the bed. His hands slowly remove his oversized T-shirt from my body.
"You know, it drove me insane the first time you said that to me..." He trails, kissing my chest.
"You walked into my classroom with that tiny skirt and my shirt on, I almost couldn't resist you then." I watch as he takes his own shirt off and I don't know how much more I can take.
I trace my fingers along his abs and watch as chill bumps rise on his skin. He lifts my thighs and wraps them around his waist, pushing himself into me.
I remove my hands from his abs and trail them down to his waistband. He's more than ready for me.
"Journie, baby." He groans. I take control and kiss him. Our mouths open and tongues intertwine, he was the most

delicious thing I've ever had.

"Stop with the teasing." He moans and I press myself harder against him. I smirk.

"I'm feeling rather torturous today." He grabs my hands and pins them above my head, and I giggle. I loved this side of him. He places rough kisses along my neck, and I almost combust then. He had a way with his hands. If it is even possible at all, I bring myself closer to him.

He grinds himself into me and I squeeze my eyes shut. I feel myself getting closer to the edge and match his rhythm. A wave of ecstasy washes over me and I collapse under him. A sinful smile appears on his lips as he wraps them back around his waist.

"I'm not done with you yet baby." I arch my hips into him again, but this time he doesn't delay me any longer and gives me exactly what I've been wanting.

Moments later, we are fully dressed and freshly showered.

"So, what do you want to eat for breakfast?" He asks and images of IHOPS fluffy pancakes fill my mind. I lick my lips.

"IHOP?" I question, throwing my wet hair into a bun.

"Sounds delicious." Aiden grabs his keys from the counter, and I follow soon after.

Once we arrive, I immediately know I want a stack of pancakes and sausage.

I don't even have to look at the menu. We give the waitress our orders and I look over to Aiden who is staring me down.

"Huge appetite?" He questions and I nod.

"Sex makes me hungry, what can I say?" I laugh and take a small sip of my coffee. Under the table I place my hand on my belly, I wish I could have told him I was really eating for two, but for now, that would have to suffice. It seemed to ease his curiosity.
As soon as the food came out and it hit my nostrils a wave of nausea rolled over me. I excused myself quickly to the bathroom, running before I threw up all over the food. Wiping at my mouth, I stand up weakly. My stomach was still protesting at me to eat. I make my way back over to the table; a concerned Aiden was staring back at me.
"Are you okay baby?" He stands up and squats beside me. I nod my head and take a bite of my delicious pancakes. Maybe I could keep it down.
"Yes."
"So, I know Halloween is coming up next week, is there anything, in particular, you want to do?" I wipe my face with a napkin and smile at him.
"Honestly, I would be okay with lying in bed with you watching scary movies and baking sweets."
"Sounds perfect." Aiden takes my hand in his and kisses it.
"Have you thought anymore about taking your position back?" I question, I didn't really want him to get too stressed about it. I knew he loved teaching there so I hoped he would take it.
"Yes. I wanted to ask your thoughts before I just jumped the gun." His blue eyes stared into mine.
I shrug my shoulders, if he wanted to take it and thought it would be safe then I was all for it. I have my application

pending for a community college for January, so I knew I wouldn't be attending NYU.
"If you think it's a good idea then I am for it. I'm no longer a student there." A big smile broke out onto his face. I could tell it made him happy.
"I'll give him a call tomorrow to let him know. I love you!" Aiden exclaims, kissing my hand one more time. I smile lovingly at him.
"I love you." I reply, finishing off my pancakes.
"Are you ready to go home and pack? If we leave within the next few hours,
we should get there before dark." He nods,
"Yes, but first I want dessert." A blush creeps onto my face and I giggle.
"It's all yours."

TWENTY:

JOURNIE

"Mom!" I exclaim and pull her into a hug. After a long two-hour car ride, I had finally made it home. She placed a light kiss on my forehead and pulled away to eye Aiden.
"Oh, come here." She smiled, pulling Aiden into a welcoming hug. I watched as he relaxed in her arms, it was thrilling to see her accept him.
She pulled away and welcomed us both in. Aiden took my bag from my hands.
"It's the first room on the right." I tell him, pointing towards the stairs. He nods his head and I turn to my mom.
"Can I talk to you alone for a minute?" She smiles at me and nods towards the table.
"Sure honey, what's going on?" I take a deep breath before sitting down, might as well get the biggest news over with.
"I'm pregnant." I say and watch as her mouth falls open and then a smile spreads across her face. She pulls me into a hug,
"I knew it wouldn't be long. Congratulations honey, I can't wait to spoil the little stinker. Does Aiden know?" I quickly shake my head,

"I was waiting to tell him on Halloween. I have something up my sleeve." I hear her laugh and can't help the giddiness that runs through me. I've known ever since I was little that I wanted to be a mother, but I didn't think it would be this soon. I turn twenty in two weeks.

"Anything else you need to tell me?" She asks, raising her brow.

"I have had a couple of more run-ins with Andrew and because of that I have decided to not finish the semester out at NYU and transfer to a smaller community college. Aiden is going to be teaching at NYU again for the spring semester."

"That's a lot for one sentence. Whatever you think is safer for you, but I really think if Andrew tries to bother you again, you need to go to the police." I nod my head. I hoped he didn't but I'm sure he had more tricks up his sleeve.

"I am. He does have photographic evidence of Aiden and I. But I'm not too worried about that, especially since Aiden is taking his position back." My mom reaches her hand out to stroke my face,

"I know baby but I'm worried about you. Always be careful and never go anywhere alone."

"I know baby but I'm worried about you. Always be careful and never go anywhere alone."

"Yeah, that rarely happens with Aiden around." I chuckle and lean on the table.

"How far along are you?"

"If I must guess, I'd say maybe five weeks. I have my first

appointment set up for next week." My mom smiles and claps her hands together.

"Oh, I'm so excited!" She pulls me into another hug, and I squeeze her tightly. Once she lets me go, I feel around in my pocket for my phone and realize it isn't there.

"I think I left my phone in the car I'll be right back." The sun has just started to set and various colors were filling the sky. I make my way outside and curse when the doors are locked. I start towards the house when suddenly a cold chill runs down my spine.

In that moment I knew he was here. I knew he was watching me. I didn't have time to react before something was wrapped around my mouth. I tried to scream but the fabric was keeping me from doing so.

"I told you, you are mine." Tears fall from my eyes as I am tossed over Andrew's shoulder. I don't even have my phone to call for help. My heart is pounding, and I feel helpless. He begins running towards what I assume is his car when I hear a loud voice shout. "PUT HER DOWN!!" I realize that voice is Aiden's and a wave of relief washes over me. Andrew doesn't listen but instead runs faster and I feel as if I'm going to fall from his grasp. The only thing I could think about was the baby. I hoped the baby would be okay.

The next thing I know, I am on the ground and my head is in searing pain. I lift my hand to grip my head as my vision goes blurry. I feel strong arms lift me up and I know by the touch it is Aiden.

"Journie baby you have to stay awake." I feel a hot wet

tear hit my face and realize it's Aiden's. He holds my head in his hands and quickly dials a number on his phone. I hear police sirens faintly in the distance. That is the last thing I remember before the world fades before me.

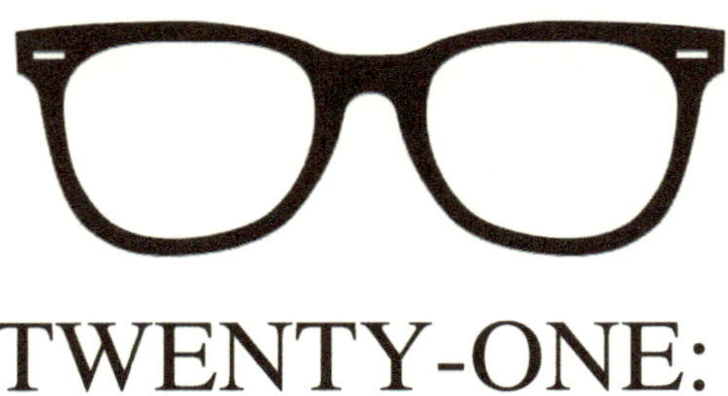

TWENTY-ONE:

AIDEN

I take Journie's hand in mine and place a kiss on it. I don't know why she would keep such a big secret from me. I stare down at the ultrasound in my hands. It all adds up now. Her being so tired, all the mornings she would wake up sick.

Though she thought I was asleep, I still heard her many mornings. All of her food aversions. I thought it was just the stress from Andrew and not a baby. I lean down and whisper in her ear,

"I love you and the baby so much. Please wake up." It had been only a few days since the incident with Andrew. It was the best feeling ever to see that bastard walking away in handcuffs. I don't expect to see him for a very long time.

I was thankful for gut feelings and the fact I listened to it this time.

If I hadn't, there is no telling what would have happened if I hadn't caught him. My stomach became nauseous just thinking about it.

I felt a light squeeze on my hand and jumped up. I watch as Journie slowly opens her eyes, and I could jump for joy.

"Aiden?" She calls in a raspy voice and I run out the door to call the nurse in.
"I'm here baby." I lean down to kiss her forehead. A small smile appears on her lips and my heart flutters. She was so perfect. I couldn't wait to spoil our mini-me. Sure, I wasn't expecting children with her this soon, but I knew it was all in God's plan.
I watch as the doctor helps her sit up and asks her various questions. Once he's satisfied and leaves the room, I notice she lays her hand on her belly.
"Is the baby okay?" I smile and pick up the ultrasound photos.
"Good as ever baby. I am over the moon! I wish you would have told me sooner."
I watch as Journie's eyes glaze over with tears and before they have the chance to spill over, I wipe at her eyes.
"It was supposed to be a surprise. I was going to tell you on Halloween." I cup both sides of her face gently and kiss her soft lips.
"That's okay baby. I'm thankful that everything is perfect."
"Where's my mom?" She questions, her eyes darting around the room.
"She stepped out to grab lunch, she should be back any minute now." I pull her gently to my chest; I was ecstatic that she was finally awake.
"Did they say when I can go home?" I shook my head, "They didn't say that. I'm hoping before Halloween so that way we can still spend the day together. I love you both so much." I place my hands gently on her stomach.

She smiles and places her hand on top of mine.
"She was truly made of love." Journie laughs and looks at me.
"She?" I question, I didn't think we could find out the gender this early.
"Yeah, just a gut feeling." She shrugged.
"I would love to have a mini you running around."
As soon as the words escape my lips, the door opens and Journie's mom walks in. She nearly drops the food when she sees Journie is sitting up.
"Journie baby! How are you feeling?" Her mom runs over to the bed and gives her a light hug.
"Other than a slight headache, I feel fine." I watch as her mom places a kiss on her forehead, and I can't help the smile that appears on my face. I was thankful Journie had a good relationship with her mom considering I never did. To me, it was the most important bond you could have.
"What happened to Andrew?" I was wondering when she was going to ask that.
"I haven't heard anything since he left in handcuffs, but my guess is that we won't hear from him until we have a court date." I hear Journie blow out a big breath. I knew she was thinking of Andrew still outing us.
"But that could be a few months away, so I wouldn't worry about that right now. All you need to focus on is relaxing and growing my beautiful grand baby." Journie's mom kissed her forehead again, and a huge smile broke out into my face.
I couldn't wait for Journie to become the best mother. Just

then a knock sounded on the door,
"Good afternoon! Ms. Journie how are you feeling?" The doctor smiled at her and as Journie replied, her whole face lit up.
"Good as new." She chuckled, placing a hand on her stomach.
"That's great to hear. So, I've got some good news for you, if all goes well this evening, by tomorrow morning you should be out of here."
"Everything looks perfectly normal, the baby is doing perfectly fine, growing as should be." I smiled at that statement; I was stoked to become a father. I couldn't have asked for a better person than Journie to have a baby with.
"Get some rest!" The doctor smiles goodbye and I walk over to Journie, bending down to kiss her forehead.
"I love you, so much."
"And I love you." She replies, meeting my lips with hers. I'll never get used to the sparks that run through me each time our lips meet. I knew I wanted to spend forever with her.
Who would have known that in just a few months, that life could change drastically. I've met my soulmate and started a family. Our time was short, but I wouldn't have it any other way.

TWENTY-TWO:

JOURNIE

The crisp cool air of January hit my cheeks as I stepped outside. I let out a huge breath as Aiden hugged me.

"We did it baby! And everything went great! That bastard got what he deserved." He leaned down to place a kiss on my cheek and then knelt down on one knee to kiss my growing belly. Pure joy flooded through me. He was going to be the best father and I couldn't wait until we had her in our arms.

We didn't find the gender out until next week, but I just knew that she was going to be a girl. Aiden hoped for a boy, naturally.

"I'm surprised he didn't threaten our relationship." I speak. I was very relieved he didn't.

"That's because he knew he was in for it either way."

Aiden scooped me into another hug and I relished in it. Every single time, I got lost in him. He was my home. He would forever be my home.

"How about we go home and relax? It's been a rough couple of weeks."

Aiden's first semester back at NYU began next week and I

have decided to do virtual classes until after the baby is born. I did offer to get at least a part-time job, but according to Aiden with his pay raise I wouldn't need to. He promised to take care of the baby and I fully. I tried to argue with him, but it got me nowhere. Arguing with him was like arguing with a brick wall.
"That sounds like a plan to me." I grab his hand as we walk to the car, proud that I was able to show him affection in public.
"Do you want to grab dinner while we are out? We can go to the diner?" He questions and I nod. It had become my favorite place to eat.
"Yes! We would greatly enjoy that!" I say and place a hand on my stomach. I was only around four months, but everyone said I looked like I was further along. You could definitely tell with my small frame that I was pregnant and I loved every second of it. The morning sickness had finally subsided and for that I was thankful.
Aiden's favorite thing to do before we fell asleep each night was talk to the baby and cradle my stomach. And I absolutely adored it.

"And the usual for you?" The waitress smiled at me and I shook my head. I was wanting something different than my usual burger.
"Actually, I'll take the loaded cheese fries and the chicken sandwich." I say, my mouth watering thinking about devouring the fries. I haven't had a good batch of cheese

fries in a long time. Right now, they were screaming my name.
"You'll be screaming mine later." Aiden winks and I cock my head to the side.
"What?"
"You said the cheese fries were screaming your name." He laughs, taking a sip of his drink. I let out a small laugh.
"Pregnancy brain." Aiden laughs at this, and I throw an unopened straw at him.
"Ah, I see you woke up and chose violence today?" He gives me a wink that makes my knees weak.
"Only for you." I shoot back, taking a sip of my cookies and cream milkshake.
"Hmmm, I like this side of you." Heat floods my face and I smile.
"Also, I love that I can still make you blush." I reach over the table and grab his hand. He lifts mine up and places a soft kiss on the back of my hand. Once all of my food is devoured, I'm ready to get home and lay down.
"Time for a nap!" I say and stand up. I stretch my arms and yawn.
"There won't be much sleeping with me around." Aiden smirks and I roll my eyes at him.
He pulls me into a tight embrace and at this moment in time, I never want to let go. He was my forever home.

TWENTY-THREE:

JOURNIE

I pull my knees up to my chest and wipe at my eyes. I really had no reason to cry. Aiden stirred in the bed beside me briefly before sitting up. He immediately pulled me into his arms.

"What's wrong baby?" I shook my head in his chest.

"I don't know. I woke up wanting some water and then I was suddenly sad." I shrug and as a chuckle left his lips.

"Strange, because I was just having a dream about you bawling. I guess my intuition kicked in and woke me up. What would make you feel better?" I shrug my shoulders again, his heartbeat calming me.

"Honestly, all I need is for you to hold me." I say as he grabs my chin and tilts my face so I'm looking into his eyes.

"That I can work with." He pulls me into his chest and places his head on top of mine.

"I love you so much." He kissed the top of my head, my stomach swarming with butterflies. He was the only one to ever make me feel this way. He was, is my one and only. I could stay in his arms forever.

"And I love you." I close my eyes and could feel myself

start to drift back off to sleep. In only a few short hours we would be knowing the gender of our baby and I couldn't wait.

"Baby! It's past noon." A whisper came near my ear, jolting me awake.
"We have to be at your mom's in three hours." I groan and roll over on my side.
"Cuddle me?" I whine and feel the bed dip beside me.
"Come here baby." I smile and move over onto Aiden's lap.
"Right where you belong." It doesn't take long for his lips to find my neck. Chills cover my body. I run my hands through his hair, earning a moan of satisfaction from him. He brings his lips up to mine, kissing me hungrily. I pulled away breathlessly.
"Soon we won't be able to be this close." I laugh and bring my hand down to cradle my stomach.
"She's going to be getting bigger."
Aiden places his hand on top of mine and I smile.
"You mean he?" Aiden counters, looking into my eyes.
"We'll find out in a few short hours." I say and place my lips back onto his. He grips the back of my neck pulling me closer to him. I would never get enough of his touch.
"As fun as this is, we need to be getting ready." I sigh as I pull away from him. A groan leaves his lips.
"Ten minutes baby, I'm not done with you yet."

I giggle as he lifts my shirt.
"I was hoping you'd say that."

I look at myself in the mirror once more before making my way outside. I bought a baby pink dress that fit all my curves just right. I was sporting my girl all the way through. Aiden on the other hand had on a baby blue button-up and khaki pants. He was bound and determined it was a boy. Of course, I would be happy either way.
"Oh baby! You look great!" My mom smiled, pulling me into a hug. She was my biggest supporter and had grown to love Aiden just as much or maybe even more than I. She kissed my cheek before pulling Aiden into another hug.
"I love you both so much!" My mom was the only one I trusted with the gender results and I knew she was already over the moon. Aiden and I had just started in the nursery last weekend and I couldn't wait to fill it with clothes and decorate it.
Once we all gather outside, my mom hands Aiden and I both a cannon. I take a deep breath before looking at Aiden. He gives me a wink and smiles. My heart melts.
"THREE, TWO, ONE!" My mom counts down and I squeeze my eyes shut before pulling the cord back. Loud booms fill the air and suddenly I am surrounded by blue smoke. I let out a happy squeal and run into Aiden's arms. He was getting his wish of a boy and I couldn't wait to have a mini Aiden running around.

"Told you!" Aiden laughed and placed a passionate kiss on my lips. I can't wipe the smile off my face.
My mom is the next to pull me into a hug.
"Have you thought of a name?" I smile over at Aiden and give him a gesture that will reveal his name. It took us many weeks to finally decide on a girl and boy name. I was in love with both.
"Noah Pierce Bennett." Aiden smiles big and leans down to kiss my stomach.
"Oh I love it!" My mom cooed. I let a big yawn escape my lips. My belly was full and I was tired. I give Aiden another hug.
"I think I'm going to go take a nap." I say and pull
My hair into a messy bun.
"Give me about ten and I'll be joining you." I narrow my eyes at him.
"No funky business. I'm tired." I say and yawn again. Napping had become my new favorite pastime. I watch as a pout settles on his lips.
"I mean it." I say as I walk into the house, strip of my dress and lay in my bed.

TWENTY-FOUR:

AIDEN

I stare at the velvet box in my palms. With shaky hands, I place it into my pocket. I told Journie to get ready and put on her most comfortable clothes. She had always wanted to go to the beach with me and I wanted to make it special for her.

She was finally nearing the end of her pregnancy and had only two weeks left to go. I knew even after dating her for a few weeks I would marry her one day. She was my perfect puzzle piece and I couldn't wait to call her my wife.

“Are you ready baby?” I ask, putting shoes on my feet. Standing up, I made sure the ring was hidden well and secured in my pocket.

Her mom thought it was a great idea and couldn’t wait.

I adored Journie's mother like she was my own. Considering my own mother wasn't the best, it was nice to have a mother figure who cared for once. I walk over to her and place my arms around her waist. A smile appeared on my lips as I felt Noah kick me. It was the best feeling in the world. I couldn't wait to have him in my arms.

"I love you so much!" She turns around and wraps her

arms around my neck.
"I love you."
I place a soft kiss on her lips and look over her outfit. Even in lounge shorts and a t-shirt she looked ready to devour. The most beautiful woman I have ever laid my eyes on.
Flickering the bathroom light off, she walked out grabbing her purse.
“I’m ready!” She squealed excitedly. I made reservations at a restaurant on the beach and I couldn’t wait for her to see the surprise I had waiting for her.
I knew her dream proposal was at the beach and I wanted all of her dreams to come true.
After half an hour and one stop to empty her bladder, we finally made it to the beach. Her face lit up as she got out of the car but quickly fell as if she was thinking something.
"Is something wrong baby?"
"I didn't bring a swimsuit." She pouted, folding her arms over her chest. I laugh and pull out a bag from my backseat.
"I've got you covered." A big smile took over her features as she threw her arms around me.
"You are the best!" She grabs both sides of my face and places a big wet kiss on my lips and I can't help but laugh when she pulls away. I loved seeing her happy.
"Why are you laughing?"
"You are just too cute." I lightly tap her nose. She scrunches her nose at me, and I can't help but reel her in

for a kiss. She snakes her arms around my neck and pulls me as close as possible to her. I loved this woman with every fiber of my being and I absolutely could not wait to make her my wife. I pulled away all too soon and place a light kiss on her forehead.
"Shall we begin?" I toss the beach bag over my shoulder as she nods her head. I grab her hand as we walk towards the changing rooms.
"Meet you out here in five!" She squeals and runs off. I laugh at her as she walks away from me, looking absolutely perfect.
"Are you ready to swim?" I ask once we find a spot to place our things.
Journie nods her head furiously.
"Beat you there." I laugh and run away from her. Once I reach the shore, I turn around and look at her steadily walking towards me, her hand on her belly.
My eyes drink her in. I don't think I've ever seen her look so good in a two-piece. Her pregnant belly made her look all the sexier and I couldn't wait to get my hands on her.
"About time, slowpoke." I tease and slap her butt. She lets out a loud squeal and I can visibly see her face become red.
"For a good reason." She laughs and takes off into the water. Once we had reached far enough for us to swim, I pull her closer to me. She wraps her legs around my waist and hands around my neck. Thankfully the waves weren't that high today. I lean forward and place a kiss on her lips. With just one simple kiss, I could show her many things

about how she makes me feel. Never in a million years would I have dreamed that I would have fallen for my student and things would work out for us.

I always told myself that was not an option, up until Journie waltzed into my life and unknowingly made me break every single rule I had for myself. Almost a year later we are expecting a beautiful baby boy and more in love than ever. I couldn't wait to have Noah in my arms.

"Are you up to try something different?" I whisper in her ear and watch as she shivers from my words. She stares deeply into my eyes.

"I'm always up for anything, as long as it's with you." She winks and brings her lips to mine once more. I loved how affectionate she was. At one time, she had admitted that her love language wasn't really affection, but I beg to differ. She always had to be touching me in some sort of way.

I pull away for a brief moment to trail kisses down her neck. She lets out a small gasp as I bite the base of her neck and wraps her legs tighter around me.

"Are you ready?" I ask, bringing my eyes back up to her. She nods. I trail my hands down and dip my fingers inside of her waist and as my fingers hit her most sensitive spot, she lulls her head back.

"Aiden, please don't stop." She moans, bringing her lips to mine. I kiss her passionately, my fingers exploring every inch of her. But I needed more. I remove my hands and press myself against her.

"Have you ever had sex in the ocean?" She shakes her

I already knew the answer.
"Then I'm glad I'm your first." I say and fill her completely.

I stare at the beautiful woman sitting in front of me. She was adamant about fixing up for dinner since it was a place I had to make reservations at. I would have been fine with her drenched hair and cute comfortable clothes. She didn't have to get dolled up for me, I thought she was perfect no matter how she dressed.
After all, the first time I met her she was wearing a pair of sweatpants and a hoodie, knowing full well it was eighty degrees outside. Even then I thought she was beautiful.
"What're you thinking?" I ask, looking down at the menu.
"Hmm, the spinach dip sounds good as an appetizer." My stomach rumbled.
"And as an entree?" She lowered her gaze at me. I could definitely go for round two.
"Probably just a hamburger." She finally shrugged.
I nervously glanced over to the patio outside. I could see the employees getting the table set up for us. I saved the best for last. The sun outside was just setting.
"Aiden?" Her soft voice snaps me out of my thoughts.
"What's up?"
"Are you ignoring me?" She chuckles and throws her straw paper at me.
"No, never." I say and look fully into her eyes.

"It seems like your were." I take her hand into mine and smile at her.
"Okay, you caught me. I was still thinking about our little rendezvous in the ocean." I watch as her cheeks turned a light shade of pink.
"Same here. Probably one of the best times we've had."
"I agree one thousand percent."
"Something we definitely have to do again." She smirks, taking a bite of her burger. Even doing that for her was graceful.
Once we finish our food, I glance back over to the patio, seeing that it was fully set up.
"Are you ready for dessert?" I watch as her tongue darts out to wet her bottom lip.
"We'll save that for later baby."
"I'm always up for dessert." I stand up and reach my hand out to her. She takes it and gives me a huge smile. My heart rate increases as we near outside. I hear a gasp leave her lips as she scans the patio before her.
"Aiden!" She squeals as her eyes wander over the terrorist. My own eyes scan over the area. Rose petals covered the floor. I place my hand on her lower back and guide her over towards the balcony. I had another surprise waiting for her. I arranged for a heart-shaped rose bed to be placed on the beach, with the words 'will you marry me?' Written in the sand.
As she looks down at the beach, she turns to me and I am already down on one knee.
"Journie, I don't really know where to start," I trail, the

tears are already streaming down both of our faces. I take a deep breath.
"I love you, so much. The first day we met, I kicked myself for not getting your number. Then by pure fate, you stepped into my classroom and stole my heart the very next day. I tried my best to stay away from you, but I couldn't. My heart is completely yours. I promise to take care of you, to cherish you, and to love you for as long as I live. Will you do me the honor of becoming my wife?"
I pull the velvet box from my pocket with shaky hands. I stand up as she throws her arms around my neck, sobbing into my neck.
"Yes!" She pulls away and holds out her hand for me to place the ring.
"I love it! And I love you even more. My heart will always be yours Aiden!" She presses her lips to mine and electricity shoots through my veins like the very first time. Even though our fates may be forbidden, she will always be the love of my life.

EPILOGUE:

JOURNIE

THREE YEARS LATER

"Mommy!" Noah squeals as he jumps into my arms.
"Daddy's being a monster again!" I turn over to look at Aiden who is hunched on the ground on all fours, a smirk on his face.

"I'll tell daddy to stop scaring you." I give Aiden a fake stern look.

"You better stop daddy!" I can't help the laugh that escapes my lips. Noah had just turned three and thought everyone was either a dinosaur or a monster. I thought it was the most hilarious thing while Aiden wasn't so amused. Though, his favorite monster was his daddy.

"Are you ready to try for another one?" Aiden stood up straight, making his way over to me. He wraps me in his warm embrace, and I melt into him.

"I would love a girl." I say and bury my head into his chest.

"I like the idea of having a mini Journie running around. I hate to break it to you, but Noah is me made over." I take a glance at our blue-eyed baby boy and smile.

"He definitely is."
"You'll get your turn." He kisses my forehead and steps away from me. I'm cold from his absence. In the three years since Aiden proposed to me, I put myself through virtual school, earning just an associate's degree in English.
It was tough with a newborn baby but with Aiden's love and support, we made it. I'm about to start my journey as an author, while Aiden is still teaching at NYU and thriving. I'd say he's doing perfect for a thirty-year-old man.
I watch as he chases Noah down the hallway and scoops him into his arms. At first, he wasn't sure he'd be the best dad but I knew from the beginning that he would be. He never once complained about having to get up in the middle of the night to tend to Noah. He was a lifesaver when I needed sleep.
I watch as he covers Noah's face in kisses and I run over to join them. They will always be my favorite boys.
I tickle Noah's stomach and he lets out a loud giggle that warms my heart.
Never in a million years would I have dreamed that I would fall in love with my professor at nineteen, it working out and marrying him. Maybe our fates weren't forbidden after all.

www.ingramcontent.com/pod-product-compliance
Lightning Source LLC
LaVergne TN
LVHW090924150826
845672LV00011B/1707

* 9 7 9 8 8 4 8 2 7 0 1 0 5 *